OBSESSION

Deadly Seven Book 1

CASSIE HARGROVE

STORY BROOKS

Copyright © 2021 by Cassie Hargrove and Story Brooks

All rights reserved.

No part of this book may be reproduced in any form or by any electronic or mechanical means, including information storage and retrieval systems, without written permission from the author, except for the use of brief quotations in a book review.

Cover Design: Cassie Hargrove and JM Designs

Introduction

Okay.

If you're a regular reader of Cassie Hargrove's, we need you to know that this is MUCH darker than anything she has ever written in the past.

This is not the sweet and loving Daddy romances you're used to from her. It's not even similar to Daddy's Little Novice and that was about a hitman kidnapping his Little.

This is dark and raw with so many triggers, you need to prepare yourself.

This is a side of Cassie no reader has seen up to this point…but we hope you stick around if you're up for it. <3

Trigger Warnings

This book contains several trigger warnings so be very very mindful of this list before entering into this story.

- non/con
- dub/con
- Voyeurism
- Blood play
- Knife play
- Murder
- Childhood sexual trauma
- Rape and talk of rape
- Violence
- Stalking

It also contains unsafe BDSM practices because the guys in this book, put simply, DO NOT GIVE A FUCK until they're with the FMC.

With this said, please make sure to do your research before even attempting anything written in these pages.

Read on fellow dark hearts and enjoy!

Character Intros

FMC: Haliee (Hal-ee) Morgan (Originally Hailey Shaw)
   - Father is Brent Morgan (Originally Brendon Shaw)

MC's:
   Lukas Michaels - Pride
   Torren Michaels - Envy
   Mathias Monroe - Sloth
   Creed Scott- Wrath
   Oliver Weever- Greed
   Corden Matthews- Lust
   Barren Matthews- Gluttony

Bad Guy: Dimitri Koschov

Torren
Prologue

Hell.

They say it's a place of fire and brimstone. A place you go when you die, but for the seven of us? That's complete and utter bullshit.

Hell is the life we were thrown into while growing up. Things only got better once we were forced into the same group home several years ago.

That's when we went from seven fucked up kids alone in the world, to a group of delinquents everyone was afraid of.

Alone, we were vulnerable. Easy targets.

Together? We became an unstoppable force that no one messed with.

We're the outcasts. The town murderers. Cross us and you're liable to end up in a shallow grave.

"Let me go!" the man screams as Creed cuts through the skin on his neck. "Please, I didn't do anything," he whimpers as the blood drips down his neck.

It's not a fatal wound.

No, Creed likes to play with his toys, causing the maximum amount of pain before he kills them.

"I sense a liar," Creed cackles like he's high as a fucking kite. He's not, at least not where drugs are concerned.

He's high on the kill. The sight of the blood, the smell of the fear permeating the air.

He won't be our first or our last.

What do you think happened to all of the people who wronged us? We couldn't let them live to hurt others like they had hurt us.

We were never going to let that happen, so we became the monsters that everyone feared.

Harm the innocent and we will hunt you down.

"Please. You have to believe me! I'm not dumb enough to cross you! That's a guaranteed suicide mission!" he screams like a little bitch as Creed's knife slices open his clothes, drawing blood from his chest along the way.

"I wish I could believe you, Pete. But just because you know it's a suicide mission to cross us, it didn't stop your urges. Did it?"

The guy visibly pales, pissing himself in the chair as he looks between us. "Wh-what are you talking about?" He's pale as fuck, and I snort while the others glare at him.

My brother, Lukas, moves to tower over him. Danger radiating off him like it's strangling the man so much he can't breathe.

"You fucked up. Just because the station has no evidence of you touching that little girl, doesn't mean we won't act," he sneers at the man in disgust before laying a punch to his gut.

That's right. Lukas, the oldest of all of us, is a cop.

This kind of thing won't stand where he's concerned. Not after what happened to me.

He swore an oath to protect this town and the victims of assholes like this guy, but sometimes the law isn't enough.

That's where we come in.

The Deadly Seven, each one of us representing a different deadly sin with our own fucked up twists.

Lukas, he's Pride. He hates himself for not knowing what happened to me when I was left with our mom, while he had a good life with our father. He prides himself on doing better, and never letting that sort of thing go unpunished again.

Creed, he's Wrath personified. The man has anger issues and it's a dangerous game with his dissociative disorder. He doesn't feel anything other than anger and hatred.

Then you have me, Envy. I hate anything and everything to do with people who think they're better than everyone else because of social standing, or thinking because they're sneaky, that they won't get caught.

We will always catch them.

"You can't be serious! What are you accusing me of?" he wheezes through the pain of my brother's repeated punches to his stomach.

"Destroying a little girl," I hiss, stepping up to him. "You think you can hurt a kid and we wouldn't find out about it? Big mistake." I lift my fist and punch him in the side of the head, knocking him out cold, and Creed whines.

"Why'd you go and do that? You know I can't have my fun when he's not conscious." He narrows his eyes at me as I roll mine.

"Because I think the rest of the guys need to be here for this. Now that he's admitted to his sins, albeit rather disgustingly," I curl up my nose at the acrid smell of piss surrounding us. "They need to be here for the reckoning."

He glares at me before letting out a growl and nodding. "Fine. Call them in. Let's give this asshole the brutality he deserves."

Hallee
Chapter One

Watching the trees zip by through the car window, I can't help thinking about what led us here.

Again.

I can't stop the feeling of hopelessness that seeps into my soul as my mind wanders back.

He found us again.

It's like no matter how hard Dad tries, the things he does to protect us, the asshole still finds us.

Dad got desperate this time, though. I really hope it buys us more time before we have to run again, but I'm not holding my breath. Even with the FBI hiding us in Witness Protection, my ability to hold hope is basically nonexistent.

"How are you doing there, Sparrow?" Dad asks me, glancing in my direction before turning his eyes back to the road.

"I'm good, Eagle. Just enjoying the peace for now," I reply with a soft smile before cringing to myself. God, I sound so ungrateful and helpless.

His face remains gentle though. "It's ok, Haliee. You're allowed to feel scared and worried. This isn't normal for a girl to go through, but look at the bright side of this. Porterville College offers classes in Psychology, and online courses in Psychopathology. I know you've been wanting to take them, and with these new identities you should finally get to live your life," he replies, giving more false hope.

I've heard the line a hundred times, so it doesn't surprise me when he mutters, "Just keep your head up for one more day, Sparrow, and we can fly away to freedom."

I don't know why I even bother trying to look forward to a happy future at this point, but for Dad? My rock and safety net through this living nightmare? I'll give it my best shot.

I give him another soft smile and turn my face back to the book I'm reading.

We've been on the road for hours now, and I'm starting to feel antsy about the long journey.

Less than two days ago, we were fine. Finally living for a minute without the fear of looking over our shoulders constantly. It was stupid of us really, because it left us vulnerable and exposed. We let our guards down and it almost cost us our lives.

I close my eyes for a second to breathe through the onslaught of memories.

I can hear the study window shattering and Dad screaming for me to hide, followed by gunshots and the sounds of a fight downstairs. I remember one of the assholes laughing and saying,

"You can't run forever, Brendon. Your daughter belongs to Dimitri. Your cunt of an ex made sure of that, and Dimitri wants his property. Now." Followed by another gunshot.

I was terrified it would end up being the moment I lost Dad. When the pounding footsteps raced up the stairs, I thought my heart would explode from fear and adrenaline. But then I heard my Dad whisper out, *"Ollie Ollie oxen free"*. It's our code phrase.

I knew at that moment I had exactly two minutes to grab my emergency bag and get to the car before we took off into the night.

This time though, I can feel the change in him.

I never question what happens to the men that

come after us, but I know the harsh reality of it in my bones no matter how badly I wish I could deny it.

Dad kills them.

I always struggle, worrying if this will be the day the police arrest him or if he'll go to prison, forever leaving me alone with those wicked men.

This time is different, though.

This time, the FBI is helping us escape with new identities and protection.

A clean slate.

Snapping back into the present, I realize that Dad has pulled over onto the side of the road. He's holding me close, whispering soft words of encouragement and safety into my hair.

I'm covered in sweat as my body shakes violently from the memories, the fear. The reminder of what my entire life has been reduced to.

I'm so sick and tired of living my life like this because my mother could only think about herself.

She owed some bad people a lot of money, and instead of trying to find it the honourable way, she chose to sell me.

My innocence and life for her slate and debt to be wiped clean.

When she found out she was pregnant with me, she wanted to abort but Dad talked her into carrying me. Once I was born, she signed over her parental rights, and Dad raised me as his own.

When it came time for her debts to be paid or her life taken, she used the only 'bargaining chip' she could think of.

Me.

What kind of parent sells their own fucking kid as a sex slave?!

"Come on, Sparrow, just breathe for me. That's my girl, you are so brave. You are doing great, sweetheart. Just breathe," Dad keeps whispering to me.

"I'm okay," I say as I take a deep breath. "I mean, I'm not okay, but I'm okay," I say, finally snapping myself out of it.

"We're five minutes away from Porterville. We have to meet with the local police and an agent once we get there. We'll go over the basics of our role in the Witness Protection Program, and then meet your handler. Can you hold strong just a bit longer before you can rest?" Dad asks.

I nod my head because honestly, I'm done with words at this point. I've never been able to be anything but strong. I can keep going a little while longer.

Dad gives me a quick hug before righting himself in his seat, and pulls back onto the road. It doesn't take long at all before we're passing the 'Welcome to Porterville' Population five hundred and forty-seven.

Damn. If I thought we had been secluded before, we were definitely doing it wrong.

This may actually give us a chance at finally living a normal life.

Taking a breath, I look around. The mountains are gorgeous where the town is directly centred in a valley below. Complete with a crystal-clear lake.

It looks almost like it was designed by God rather than man. Like it belongs in a fairy-tale, not the real world.

Dad follows the winding road toward the town's main street, and even though there isn't much here, I can easily see ourselves building a forever life here. As long as Dimitri stays away this time.

Pulling up in front of the police station and shutting off the car, Dad turns to me.

"This will be quick, Sparrow. After, we can grab a bite to eat at the diner and go to the cabin."

At the mention of food, my stomach reminds me that I've barely eaten these past couple of days by letting out a loud growl, and Dad smiles at me knowingly.

Getting out the car to make our way in, I turn back quickly to grab my bag from the back seat. It will give me a little something to fiddle with while we undoubtedly go through another round of interrogations.

Before I shut the car door, I notice a man in a hoodie standing in the alley across the street. His piercing eyes scream danger, and a shiver runs down my spine.

Quickly shutting the door, I run back to where Dad is waiting for me before turning to look back at the guy in the shadows again, but he's gone.

Shrugging it off, I decide that the massive amount of stress my life is currently in, is enough to dwell on without adding a creepy shadow guy to the mix.

I follow Dad into the police station so we can get this over with. Now that he's mentioned food, I find myself dying to get my hands on a juicy burger. Especially after my meltdown in the car.

I'm so lost in my thoughts of food and meltdowns, I don't see the guy standing ahead of me until I'm running right into him.

Strong hands shoot out and grab my arms to steady me as I gasp in shock.

Lukas
Chapter Two

F uck, this woman is beautiful.

Clumsy, but so fucking beautiful it makes my eyes hurt.

I'm supposed to be meeting the kid I'm going to be protecting while undercover, but it seems they're late. Not a great start for WPP.

The girl in my arms is barely over five feet tall, long wavy brunette hair, and large innocent eyes that have me wanting to wrap her up and protect her with my life like it's my sworn duty.

Which is fucked because I've never felt such a strong need to protect a stranger before. At least, not a stranger that isn't a kid my brothers and I are getting revenge and justice for.

"You okay?" I ask.

She looks up, her doe eyes blinking behind long lashes, and I have this feeling of rightness land in my chest before someone clears their throat, drawing my attention away from her beautiful face.

"Hi," she whispers.

The man's eyes narrow on my hands holding the girl and I clear my throat, checking to make sure she's sturdy before letting her go, my hands feeling too empty all of a sudden.

"Yeah, hi." His jaw grinds, and I look between him and the girl. He seems a bit old for her, but maybe he's her boyfriend?

God, I hope not.

"Dad!" she hisses under her breath, and I have to stop myself from smirking. She's cute when she blushes. "Don't be rude."

He grunts, but his eyes soften as he looks at her. It's easy to tell she's the centre of his world.

"Wasn't trying to be, Sparrow. Just tired." He gives her a small smile and she nods in acknowledgement before he turns back to me, his eyes telling me he knows exactly what was running through my mind as I looked at her.

Like I give a fuck what he thinks.

"Can you lead us to Detective Michaels? We

have a meeting with him and the Chief of Police." Shit. He's looking for me?

"I'm Detective Michaels." I watch him narrow his eyes further, fighting to not roll mine at his overprotective bullshit.

Though, if I had a daughter who looked like her, I would be a little overbearing too. She's stunning enough to pull the attention of every psycho and player in the world. Even I'm not immune to a beauty like hers.

She elbows her father in the stomach, and he lets out a puff of air before holding out his hand.

"Perfect. I'm Brent, and this is my daughter, Haliee."

Alarm bells start ringing in my head. This undercover operation I'm supposed to be helping with isn't for a kid after all, but for this gorgeous woman in front of me.

Shit. How old is she, anyway? They never filled me in on her age, just asked for someone to volunteer to watch out for her, and protect her at all times when she's away from the house. They'd said a kid was in danger and needed protection.

I'd say they misused the word kid, because she is most definitely too old to be classified as a child.

"Right," I clear my throat as I step to the side.

"It's right down here if you want to follow me." I exchange a quick look with Haliee before moving away, not waiting to see if they are following or not.

Knocking on the Chief's door, I don't wait for him to answer before opening it. Holding the door open for the girl and her father, I follow them in, closing it behind us.

Inside the office, Chief Peterson and the FBI guy are sitting, waiting.

"Ah, there you both are." FBI Agent Michael Daniels stands to shake hands with Brent before his eyes travel over Haliee's body with clear intent.

I instantly want to stand in front of her and beat the fuck out of the guy for even looking at her, but I hold my ground.

Whatever the fuck has come over me needs to settle down because it's my job to protect her. I can't do that properly if I'm thinking with my ego and dick instead of my brain.

Brent seems to catch the guy checking out his daughter as well because he moves in front of her like I wanted to, and gives Agent Daniels a scathing look that has him swallowing and sitting his pathetic ass back down in the chair.

"Sorry we're a bit late." He grabs his daughter's

hand and pushes her to sit in the only open chair, and I feel a surge of pride. He's a good father to her. When I'm not watching her, he will protect her at all costs. "We haven't slept much in the past couple days," he explains, and the Chief nods in understanding.

"That's to be expected after everything you both have gone through."

I stand guard at the door, taking everything in as they talk about where they're staying and their new identities, which are extremely close to their birth names. At least the first names are.

It's a technique I think is completely idiotic if you're trying to fucking hide someone, but I understand where they're coming from in the sense it will be easier for them to remember.

Haliee Morgan was originally Hailey Shaw, and her father was originally Brendon.

It's not a bad change of name I suppose, but I still don't like it. It feels way too similar, especially her name being so close.

However, it's not my place to say anything. I'm here to look after her and shadow her as a friend on campus. That's all.

I knew I would be watching a kid in school, but I thought they had meant elementary school. I didn't get the chance to ask many questions since it all came about so suddenly.

Hell, I haven't even told the guys yet. Chances are, they are going to lose their shit over my going undercover.

Fuck.

The second they see Haliee, they are going to be all over her. They don't trust anyone new coming into town, and there is only so much I'm going to be allowed to tell them. This went from a simple protection job to a clusterfuck in a matter of seconds.

By the time everyone has gone over everything, Haliee looks like she's about to fall asleep, but any little noise she hears has her practically jumping out of her skin, and I don't like it.

The second I get her home and settled, I'm going to sit in my car and read over her file in detail, so I know exactly what I'm up against with this.

A girl doesn't jump at everything for no reason, and they sure as hell don't end up in WPP without reasonable belief their safety is in danger.

It doesn't take us long to get into our vehicles,

and I follow them to the cabin, grinding my teeth every second of the trip.

They stopped at a diner in town and ordered some takeout before heading the rest of the way, but it was long enough for me to see him.

Of course, Mathias was watching us. My phone is repeatedly going off with questions I can't fully answer, too.

Mathias is the watcher in our group.

He sees everything that happens in our town. A lot of people think he's mute and lazy, so he was dubbed Sloth, but the fucker just doesn't talk to anyone outside of our group.

He's not lazy, either. He just prefers to watch and remember. To listen.

He only gets involved in the beatings and torture when it's absolutely necessary.

I'm not really surprised he was watching because it's what he does. What did catch me off guard was Haliee's ability to sense his eyes on her.

I watched her look around everywhere for him, knowing she was being watched. She didn't find him, but the fact that her senses are that acute will go a long way in keeping her safe throughout whatever happens next.

Mathias

WHAT THE HELL is he up to?

Whatever it is, he hasn't let us in on the secret yet, and that's worrisome. It means he's acting without thinking or having the time to think.

Lukas is smart and I trust him with our lives, but this girl he's with? I've never seen her before, and he couldn't take his eyes off of her.

She looks like some sort of angel with her long brown hair. So tiny and fragile like she could break if the wind blew too hard against her, but there was something else. Something darker and stronger.

I'm not sure if I trust her.

Lie.

I don't trust anyone outside of my brothers for good reason.

Whatever darkness she has in her, we will get it out and assess if she's a threat.

I send the guys a message about the new girl and Lukas being attached to her somehow, before putting my phone away, and head to another one of my watch spots to see if I can learn anything else we can use.

I enjoy being the watcher. The one nobody pays attention to, but I see it all. I see every sin they commit, and if it's bad enough, my brothers and I will extract their debt. Usually with their life.

I hope that angel isn't against us. It would be a shame to kill something so beautiful.

Haliee
Chapter Three

By the time Lukas leaves, I am beyond beat.

I know that I shouldn't get comfortable here because it never lasts, but for tonight, we are safe and can sleep without worry.

Something about Agent Daniels has me on edge. I can't put my finger on it, but he definitely puts the sl in sleaze.

"Hey, Dad, can I talk to you a second?" I ask him as he brings the last of our bags in.

Another thing we've learned over the years? Travel light, and don't get sentimental. Nothing lasts, and you can't always take everything with you.

"Sure, Sparrow. What's up?" I roll my eyes at his constant attempts to 'be cool'. But he is cool.

He's the best person I have in my world, and the only one I trust.

He's given up everything just to keep me out of the hands of Dimitri. I will never be able to pay Dad back for everything he's done for me, and I can't imagine my life without him in it.

Walking over to him, I pull him into a tight hug, and he sighs, relaxing around me like I'm his safe space, his home.

We need each other.

"I don't know if I trust Agent Daniels," I tell him quietly as I continue to hug him.

He snorts. "Yeah, I'm not sure I trust the guy either. But that kid seemed to be on the level."

I cringe at his calling Detective Michaels a kid. The guy is only about ten years older than me if I had to make a guess.

He's also built like a brick wall. Running into him can easily be counted as one of my topmost embarrassing moments to date.

On top of his being older, he also happens to be one of the sexiest guys I have ever seen in my life. All tall and masculine with dirty blonde hair and striking blue eyes. He's essentially sex on a stick.

Not that I'd know what sex is like, but he's the first guy I've ever been remotely attracted to.

This can't end well.

He's going to be with me every day acting as my shadow while I'm at school or shopping. The simplest plan is to pretend like he's my boyfriend while we're out in public.

That's what we had decided on, or rather had been decided for us. Lukas is well known to the locals, so he can't exactly fly under the radar against them. I just hope Dimitri's men don't come here.

The more people involved, the more chances of someone I care about getting hurt.

"Yeah, he seems nice," I say as I pull back, and Dad grunts.

"He could do without checking you out while I'm around."

I snort this time. "Dad, it's not like that. He's just taking the job of protecting me seriously. I think it's a good thing."

He looks at me with a serious expression before giving a curt nod. "You're right. I think this is going to be good, Haliee." He gives me a small smile that I easily return.

"I hope so, Brent," I mock his new name, and he sighs.

"Just promise to not let your guard down. Even if Daniels is trustworthy, we aren't completely hidden," he warns, and I nod, the anxiety still running through me.

"I know, Dad. I promise I will always be on guard. Promise me you'll do the same?"

He pulls me in for another hug and nods.

"Promise, baby girl. Now, let's get some rest. For tonight, we're safe. Let's relax, okay?"

I nod, and say my goodnights, heading into my room to get ready for bed.

It doesn't take more than a few minutes before I'm passed out hard from the stress of the last couple days catching up with me.

Oliver

. . .

"Creed, wait!" I shout in desperation. Not that I don't want this, because I really fucking do, but this is our game.

This is how we cope with the shit that haunts us.

He needs prey, and I'm more than willing to play the part. I will never fail to make sure these guys, these demons I'm joined to, never want for anything.

"I said shut the fuck up, and roll the fuck over, Ollie," Creed growls out. His eyes are all black at this point, showing his true nature. His hands grab me around my thighs, rolling me over with as much violence as possible.

I know he wants the fight. He needs it.

I kick out at him, still playing his little scared mouse which only fuels him more.

"NO! Get the fuck off me!" I yell out.

I scramble into a position on my hands and knees in an attempt to run from him. A mistake on my part, really. One should know never to turn their back on a predator.

Before I can even move an inch, his naked body drapes over me, wrenching my hands out from under me. Holding them behind my back, he grabs his belt from the floor, securing me in place.

His hands move down the globes of my ass and part my cheeks.

"Fuck, man, at least use lube and prep me this time. You fucked me up for almost a week last time, and I couldn't sit down right." My voice is muffled by the bed, but I really don't care either way he chooses to take me.

He grabs me by the hips and jacks my ass in the air. Splaying my legs on either side of his, I sigh in relief when I hear the blessed sound of a lid cracking open, followed by the freezing cold lube hitting the crack of my ass. Before I can even enjoy the fact he's using lube this time, I feel a sharp sting on my thigh, and Creed starts laughing like the fucking lunatic he is.

"You look good like this, Ollie. All bound up and at my mercy with blood dripping down your thigh from my blade. I wonder if you like the pain too? Is that why you let me defile you like this? It gets you fucking high, doesn't it? Knowing I can give you what you truly need, and feed your helpless desires," Creed groans into my ear.

I suck in a sharp breath when I feel his hand move to the cut he made on my leg. He quickly gathers some blood before moving his hand to my dick, pumping my length and drawing a long, tortured moan from my chest.

"You feel that, Ollie? That's me owning you with the simplest touch. But you already know I'm not here for your pleasure right now. You'll cum, but only by yourself. No hands, no rubbing this dick against the covers. Nothing. You'll cum with my dick in that tight ass, won't you?" Creed's filthy words barely filter past the pleasure he's giving me.

He removes his hand from my cock, and I almost whine out at how desperate he has me. His fingers trace down my spine before trailing them down to my ass. He parts my cheeks again, and I jump when I feel those same deadly fingers start to massage my puckered hole.

I feel like I'm about to combust as it is, so when he eases his finger into my tight space, my eyes start to roll into the back of my head. Thank fuck he's not in a bad mood and is taking the time to prep me.

Last week, he came home pissed and raging over Torren knocking out his toy before he had his fill of him.

I remember him smashing through the door and tearing my shirt off with his fucking teeth. Using my ripped shirt to restrain me, he bent me over, a quick spit-shot hitting my hole before he rammed his thickness into me. The fucking pain was nearly unbearable to the point I almost passed out.

Creed bends over and starts kissing down my spine while adding in a second, then third finger. I know this is his way of making it up to me by being his version of gentle. Even if he'll need new sheets tomorrow from my blood ruining them.

I feel him remove his fingers, and brace myself. The crown of his cock is against my tight hole but before he can slam home inside me, someone starts pounding on the bedroom door.

"Creed, Ollie, meeting in the living room right now!" Mathias bellows from the other side of the door. For such a quiet guy, something's got him in a tizzy.

"Fuck, five minutes, Matty boy!" Creed yells back before inching his way into me, making me groan.

"No, right now. Lukas just got here, and we all need to talk," Mathias hollers, before pounding on the door again.

"I'm going to plow into this ass when we're done, Ollie. You better be prepared for me," Creed whispers in my ear, causing me to shiver. He withdraws his cock and starts untying my hands.

I rub my wrists out before leaning over and grabbing the first aid kit under my nightstand.

I started keeping one there when I figured out really quick that Creed needed pain with his pleasure. Even though he cut me, he would have ended up cutting himself or having me do it in order get his release.

I gently start cleaning up the cut, applying ointment and a bandage to it while Creed gets dressed. I go to grab for my boxers when Creed grabs my wrist and drags me to him.

"Ollie, you make the monsters disappear for a minute when I'm with you like this," he tells me gently, before leaning down for a kiss.

It's sweet but cold. Just like him.

He lets me go and walks out the bedroom door leaving me to stare at his retreating back.

I shake off the bizarre encounter because Creed isn't soft, or gentle. Something is messing with his head a lot today.

Getting dressed quickly, I head out to the living room where all the guys are currently sitting, leaning against the wall, or if you're Creed, crouched on the fucking counter playing with a blade making little cuts to the pads of his fingers.

I walk over next to Lukas and sit down.

He looks rough. I've never known this man to be anything but calm, so seeing him like this I know something is definitely up. I'm just about to turn my attention to Mathias, but the gleam of Lukas' gun catches my eye.

My demon starts whispering sweet nothings through my mind and I can see where this piece of steel would be useful. They don't call me Greed for nothing.

I take what I want and offer no apologies for it. I'm sure Torren would benefit more from this than Lukas will, and I'd do anything for these guys.

"Hey, Lukey, what the fuck is that on the lawn?" I say, pointing out the window. His head snaps in that direction and I move in. Sliding my hand across the cushions while keeping his attention on nothing, I unbutton the holster, and gently start sliding the gun from its resting place.

Oh yeah, this is going to be nice on Torren. My demon is already doing a little victory dance in my head.

I just about have the gun completely out when my wrist is snatched up causing me to drop it back into the holster. Lukas turns his head back to me slowly while Torren holds my hand up. I give them both a toothy smile before I try to dart off the couch and save my life.

The motherfuckers dogpile me before I get two feet in front of me, and start pounding on my ribs.

Torren

MOTHERFUCKER HAS LOST HIS MIND.

Seriously? How did Ollie ever expect to get away with taking Lukas' piece? I'm surrounded by fucking insanity, I swear.

"You fucker! What the hell were you thinking? That's my work piece!" Lukas growls, wrapping his arm around Ollie's neck in a sleeper hold.

"Do I really even need to answer that?" he sasses back, and I roll my eyes.

Fucking idiot.

"My work gun is off limits, and you fucking well know it, shithead!" Lukas gives one more squeeze around his neck before releasing him and standing back up. "Unless you fuckers want me to lose the ability to cover up the shit we do?" he questions, and we're all quiet.

It's not a secret that we get away with all the killing because Luke has a way of making evidence disappear. Pissing him off or getting him fired would only hinder our progress.

"That's what I thought," he huffs before dropping back onto the couch.

Mathias has something up his ass, and he's glaring at my brother like he's wronged him in some way.

What the fuck is that about?

"What the hell is going on?" I ask, sitting down beside Luke as Creed jumps off the counter, licking the blood from his fingers.

Fucking nutcase. He doesn't care whose blood it is, he just needs to be surrounded by it at all times.

"Ask your brother," Mathias all but growls, his glare never once leaving Luke.

"Spying on me, Mathias?" my brother questions him.

"Not purposely. What were you doing with that woman, huh? I've never seen her before."

My eyebrows shoot into my hairline. I've never seen my brother with a chick, not one where he's doing something worth questioning.

"She's my job," he states, and we all look to him in confusion. With a sigh, he continues. "It was a last-minute job from the FBI. I can't get into a lot of details, but I'm officially undercover with her from this moment on," he states.

"Undercover?" Barren sits up straighter.

"Yeah. I'm officially a college student." He rolls his eyes. School is not his forte. "I'm going to become a close friend and stick by her side whenever she's away from the house. Basically, I'm her official bodyguard/babysitter," he groans, and I can't help but laugh.

"Why?" I ask and he glares at me before something dark passes his gaze.

"I wasn't given many facts when I volunteered. Just that some sick fuck is after a kid, and she needed protection until the guy is caught," he sighs, and my gut churns.

We've all been the subject of some dark and twisted shit as kids. Lukas would do anything to protect a kid…but Mathias said a chick?

"That was not a kid," Mathias points out as though he's reading my thoughts.

"No shit," Luke growls, rubbing his hand down his face like he's exhausted. "I was just as surprised as you were when she ran into me." He shakes his head. "But it was too late. I had already volunteered, and the girl is tiny. If someone really is after her, she's going to need the protection. No way can she defend herself."

There's a dark cackle behind us, and we all let out a collective groan.

"Defenceless toy?" Creed's smile is other worldly dark, and Luke growls.

"Don't even fucking think about it." He's awfully defensive of a stranger. We don't even know her or if she can be trusted.

"You don't know anything about her. She can't be trusted," Corden glowers as Mathias nods in agreement.

As the Deadly Seven, we're all sketchy about new people in our town. It doesn't happen often, but when it does, we are all over their business, trying to find out if they're friend or foe. Nine times out of ten, they all have something to hide.

"Oh, I will think about it. Mathias, show me where she lives." Creed smiles wide, and I have to hold Luke down from attacking him.

"Settle the fuck down, Luke," I warn him. "What the fuck has gotten into you?"

He glares at me. "Since when do we taunt

women, huh? She's fucking innocent!" he snaps, and the other guys get pissy.

I can tell it's going to be a free for all soon if we don't get this shit under control.

"Enough!" Mathias hollers, and we all turn to him. He doesn't generally take charge of a situation because that's Luke's job.

Mathias is the quiet one, but Luke seems to be missing a few screws over this girl, so I guess it's up to us to pick up the leadership slack.

No one can go under the radar. We have to be on top of it, especially if Luke is going to be blind to it all.

"We do not know her. We will watch her like we do every newcomer whether you like it or not." He shoots a dark look at my brother before continuing. "Creed, stay the fuck away from her. You don't have the ability to not play with pretty things."

Creed groans, adjusting his hard-on with the same hand holding the knife, and I cringe. That's way too close for comfort.

"Ooo, a pretty toy?" He looks so excited, and I blow out a frustrated breath, about to get up before Oliver moves to stand in front of him.

"Don't even think about it, Creed. Wait for the go ahead from Matt before playing. If she's innocent, you will only hurt her and hate yourself." He pouts at Ollie.

"I want to play. If she's pretty, I bet she will bleed and scream like a fucking angel." He bites his lip. "I want a Doll, Ollie. Let me play."

Ollie shakes his head, turning back to Mathias. "I'm taking him out of here for the rest of this conversation. He needs to expel some demons before he takes this seriously. Update us later?"

Mathias looks between the two of them before he gives a sharp nod, and Ollie leads the psycho fuck out of the room.

"If any of you so much as touch her, you will have me to deal with. Be fucking warned," Luke snarls at those of us remaining, and I swallow a groan.

It's going to be a long fucking night.

Haliee
Chapter Four

Dad and I have been here for a week now, and things have finally started to settle down. We even went grocery shopping which was a big indication we felt safe enough to stay in one place for a while.

For the first several days, we ate at the local diner, not sure if we felt like we could stay. But the second he pulled into the grocery store, it was like I could let out the breath I was holding.

Knowing he has no plans of running makes life a little easier for both of us, and I think I have Lukas to thank for Dad feeling so comfortable this quickly.

The only downside is I still can't shake the feeling that I'm being watched.

Everywhere I go, even when I'm in my room at night, I feel eyes on me. They're cold, dark, sinister. And always watching.

Lukas has been like a dream this week, though. He helped Dad find a little side job even though we don't really need the money. He said it would be good to keep busy and keep our minds off things that we shouldn't be worried about with him here to guard us.

When we went to campus to register for all the classes I wanted to take, he registered with me. When I showed genuine shock, he just shrugged it off saying it was easier to do his job of protecting me if he was by my side anywhere and everywhere.

It's smart and makes sense, but I still felt kind of sad that it was because I was a job to him and nothing else.

Yeah, I know it sounds crazy, but a part of me had butterflies of hope that it could change.

Until now, Dad has been the only one to ever make me feel truly protected. Like I mean something to him.

Lukas is hot, and he's the type of guy who is

more than aware of it. I can't pretend that his flirtations don't affect me, but I won't take it to heart. I can't.

I can't settle down and have a relationship, anyway. We never stay anywhere for long.

I do feel kind of bad, though. Psychology doesn't really seem to be something a guy like Lukas would find enjoyment in, so sitting in classes with me is going to be boring as hell for a guy like him... but I'm thankful anyway.

Being a psychologist has long been a dream of mine. I want to understand the inner workings of people's minds so I can figure out why my mother would set me up for a life of torture and abuse.

Something has to be wrong with her for her to do something like that.

BY THE TIME we get to campus, I'm already a nervous mess, and trying to not let it show.

Those fucking eyes are on me again. Always on me, like I can't escape from them.

Has Dimitri found me already? The thought sends a shiver of panic down my spine.

I know it's not just the extra police presence in

the distance either. It feels like whoever is watching me wants to hunt me. That doesn't seem like Dimitri's game.

When he finds us, he moves in on us without question every time. I think it's why we're always on edge, because he doesn't give us the chance to sense his presence first. At least, not long enough to respond to it.

Over the years, I've learned to sense when I'm being watched, but him and his men move so quickly, I don't have time to really come to terms with it before they attack.

This feels different. Like I'm the prey in some sicko's game of catch me if you can.

I know I should probably tell Lukas, but I'm not sure I fully trust him yet. He's good at doing his job, but would he trust my instincts? Or would he see me as some little girl who needs saving? A little girl paranoid as fuck of the outside world.

He'd be wrong.

There's one thing no one knows about me, and I will keep it close to my heart. Dad taught me how to use a knife. I'm more skilled in self-protection than anyone would ever assume by looking at me.

If someone gets close enough, I won't go down

without a fight. I will punch, kick, and stab any son-of-a-bitch who even tries.

"You ready for this, Scratch?" Lukas gave me the nickname early on saying I'm like a cat. Cute as hell, but if I'm pushed, he bets my claws will come out.

He's not wrong.

"Shouldn't I be asking you that? It's not like this is going to be fun for you," I state, and he shrugs, giving me that million-dollar smile of his.

"Meh, maybe I will learn something. Besides, kid, protecting you is all I care about." He wraps his arms around my shoulders, pulling me into a tight side hug. It's all for show.

Everyone here needs to think we're close because he's eventually going to be my 'boyfriend'. It saves people from asking questions that way.

"Maybe you will, maybe you won't." I laugh, pulling away from his side. Being close to him does something to me that I'm not used to. It's like his touch lights me on fire from the inside out.

I know I've read about attraction and sex in books, but it's not something I've ever lived through.

"Also, stop calling me kid. You're what? Ten years older than me? Give me a break." I play punch him, and he pretends to be wounded as we both laugh walking into class.

When I sit down, he chooses the seat beside mine while the other students clamour into the room before the teacher arrives.

I've gotten almost everything out of my bag and set to take notes when I feel Lukas stiffen beside me.

Something in the air shifts. "You okay?" I ask, looking over to him before scanning the room and coming to a stop on a couple of guys watching us.

They're definitely twins, and hot as fuck, too. The one is glaring at us like we've wronged him, while the other one is looking at me like I'm some sort of popsicle he wants to lick. Or like a kid in a candy shop who wants all the things.

Gross.

I mean, okay, he's hot but I'm not really up for being objectified like that and that guy screams sex appeal the way some scream psycho killer. I can only imagine how much of a player he is.

No thank you. I'm definitely not the type of girl who wants to be another notch on someone's belt. Hard pass.

The "lustful" looking twin winks at me before turning around to face the front of the class. I can't help the blush that hits my cheeks over it. I chance a glance to the side at Lukas, and he's staring daggers at the back of the twins' heads. He's clenching his jaw tightly, and balling up his fists in an attempt to hold in whatever he's feeling right now, and it worries me a little.

He must know them to have such a strong reaction, but I shrug it off and pull the last of my supplies out of my backpack. It isn't long before the professor walks in and gets our lesson started.

Corden

THE OLD-ASS PROFESSOR is droning on about the syllabus and classwork expectations, and Barren is twitching beside me from the need to go for a run. Fucker can't sit still at all. He's always moving.

Why he decided to join me in boring classes is beyond me.

Hell, I just took this class to spy on Luke and the hot chick.

I smile to myself turning my thoughts over to the bombshell beauty taking up residence behind us. That dark raven hair and those pouty lips were enough to make my dick want to bust out of my zipper to say hi. I bite my lip to cool the burning lust running through my veins at the mere thought of her.

Fuck, how long has it been since I got my dick sucked? One, two hours? I don't know. Just another face, just another hole to bury myself in. And I'm far from being biased on which gender it is.

No wonder Lukas is keeping that tiny little sex kitten away from us. We'd break her delicate self. Barren and I weren't even supposed to be in this class, but when we saw them arrive on campus for registration, we couldn't resist changing courses to get a better look at what has Lukas so tied up in knots.

Mathias is going to go ape shit over this. Then again, he hates everyone and only barely tolerates us half the time.

Lukas looked like he was half a second away from drawing his gun and shooting us. I couldn't resist giving his obsession a tiny wink and side smile. That shit can melt the panties off of devoted married women, so I knew it would have beauty back there blushing.

I look back over at my brother, and it looks like he's about to come out of his skin. I told him he wouldn't be able to handle sitting in a room like this for long periods of time, but the dumbass insisted he was fine.

Ever since the quiet Mathias, and the steadfast Lukas got into a spat over beauty back there, we've all been on edge.

Too many times have we had to handle the filth that's come into this town. This chick is no different.

Everyone has monsters in their closets and it's us that have to exterminate them.

Each one of us brings baggage from our childhoods that have molded us into the absolutely terrifying bastards we are today.

Game on, beauty. I hope you're ready for the beasts that are watching you.

Barren

THIS ROOM IS GETTING SMALLER by the minute. My skin feels tighter, and my legs won't stop shaking. The voices in my head keep getting louder and louder. I can normally go on a run or lift weights to quiet them down. But sitting at this desk? My brother was right. I can't handle this.

What the fuck was I thinking getting involved in

this spat between Luke and Matt anyway? Oh, I know. I was thinking I could be the calm voice of reason for once.

That, and I can't trust my brother around anything with a mouth, so I had to keep an eye on him.

Fuck, the moment we got a look at them across campus, I swear Cord was about to bust a nut. I think we stopped at least three times that day to get his rocks off.

For fuck's sake. I need to get out of this damn classroom. I'm studying fitness and nutrition. I don't need this psychology shit.

I also don't need Luke shooting my brother in the head for being a tool, so I'm stuck.

This is bullshit. Why do I have to be the calm in this fucking storm?

Give me an open track, a pool or gym, and I'm happy.

Give me candy and my favourite foods; I'm happy.

Sit me in a classroom listening to some old prick talk about psychology? No.

My heart is racing, I'm sweating through my shirt, and I feel like I'm about to commit a mass murder or pass the hell out. Which one comes first is beyond me.

"That's it for today, everyone. See you next class!" The professor is excited like we all give a fuck about being here.

We don't.

"I'm getting the fuck out of here. Now!" I seethe at Cord as I pull him up from his chair and drag his ass through the door.

"Hey, wait!" A sweet voice calls out to us from behind, and Luke's growl is undeniable. I stop, turning to face this girl who must have a death wish. That's the only thing I can think of as to why she'd want to talk to someone who looks ready to kill.

"What?!" I snap, my brother looking at her like she's the next hole to fuck. He'll probably get it, too. Poor thing doesn't stand a chance against Lust.

That's who Cord is between us. He has an addiction to sex and uses it as a coping mechanism. Hell, the guy can charm fucking nuns out of their vow of celibacy.

Me? I'm Gluttony. I overdo everything I enjoy.

Workout? LOTS, it's my stress relief.

Sweets and junk food? Love them. If I wasn't a gym rat, I'd probably be well over three hundred pounds, I'm sure.

The girl flinches at my sharp tongue, and I scoff.

We will fucking eat her for breakfast and still need a solid meal after.

"Here." She takes off a black bead bracelet and shoves it into my hand with as much force as she can muster.

"What the fuck is this?" I scowl down at the jewelry like it's offensive, and she lets out a little growl of her own.

Kitty has claws? Cute.

"It's a black lava bracelet. It has calming properties to it. You can even add essential oils. I saw you fidgeting." She shrugs. "I have major anxiety too. Thought it would help." She walks off without another word, Luke glaring at us like he's about two seconds away from strangling us both.

What the fuck was that?

As though he can read my thoughts, Cord laughs.

"Cute bracelet, dude."

I groan and shove the thing in my pocket. I won't admit it to anyone else, but I'm going to look into this shit. I need something to help.

But why did she give it to me? She doesn't know me, and I was far from friendly to her.

If she could see my anxiety, that means I really

need to get control of myself. Letting others see your vulnerabilities makes you a target.

This girl is dangerous. She definitely has to go.

Haliee

"You seem to know them," I say as Lukas walks beside me.

"I know pretty much everyone in this town."

I nod, keeping my eyes on the ground. "You weren't happy they were in the class. Are they bad news?"

He takes an audible breath before blowing it out. "I wouldn't say they're bad people, just different. They're friends of mine, but I'm undercover. I got nervous."

I look at his face to see if he's telling the truth, and nod. He doesn't seem like he's lying to me. "I'm sorry my issues are causing problems for you." I really do feel bad.

Dad and I should have just kept running. He opens his mouth to speak before a squad of barbies stop in front of me.

I've seen *Mean Girls*. I know where this is going.

"Look, fresh meat." The main girl eyes Lukas before turning back to me. "Corden is mine. If you know what's good for you, you'll stay the fuck away from him."

I sigh. "Seriously? This isn't high school. Also, who the fuck is Corden?"

Lukas snorts out a laugh and the head girl steps closer.

"Amber, back the fuck off and go be a bitch to someone else." Another girl, small like me with dark red hair and glasses steps up to my side, totally getting in the other woman's face.

Nice.

Amber and her friends glare at the girl before shooting me an evil look and walking away.

Can I have her superpowers? Damn.

"You have to tell me how you did that, oh wise one."

She chuckles at me and holds out her hand. "Hi, I'm Kristen. You must be the newbie. Dad told me you were coming."

I open and close my mouth before Lukas bends and whispers in my ear.

"Kristen Carmichael. She's the Dean's daughter." I swallow and give him a small smile.

"Hey, I'm Haliee. It's nice to meet you." I shake

her hand and she smiles before linking her arm in mine.

"Nice to meet you too. I think we're going to be besties."

Well, alright then.

Hallee
Chapter Five

Classes are going relatively smooth and before I know it, an entire month has passed by. My heart is growing attached to this place. It's making it difficult for me to imagine having to run again.

Lukas has stayed by my side this whole time with the utmost patience and kindness, and I'd be lying if I said it was just this little mountain town that I'm growing attached to.

He never makes me feel like I'm a burden to him, and seems to actually enjoy being around me. The feeling is definitely mutual.

Fuck, I've been so tempted to lean over and kiss him more times than I can count since we met. We met under the worst of circumstances, but I can't shake this feeling that he's important to my life, my future.

We haven't kissed as a part of our 'cover' yet, either. So far, we are still just really great friends. But as time goes on, and the town regulars notice him spending more and more time with me, I know it's going to come.

Things with Kristen have been going surprisingly well, too.

She's not someone I would have normally chosen to attach myself to since she's so bubbly, but I find I'm really enjoying her company. I've never had a girlfriend before, and I'm glad she's my first.

She's been staying true to her word, too. We are definitely best friends. Even Dad seems to approve of her 'positivity'.

I just barely get off a video call with her before there's a knock on my door frame.

"Hey, Scratch," Luke says as he walks into my room, plopping down on the bed.

"Why are you in my room?" I raise my eyebrow in question because he's never really been up here before. And he looks nervous.

"Ah, yeah." He clears his throat with a cough. "Your Dad let me up before he left for work a few minutes ago."

I nod, knowing Dad trusts him to protect me. Would he still if he knew the kind of feelings I was having toward him? "Okay, and?" I ask, hands on my hips as I stare down at his giant frame on my double bed.

Jesus, the guy is built like a damn brick house. He's never going to fit with me in that thing.

Whoa. Slow down, Haliee. Don't even go there. You're a virgin who's never even been kissed. The chances of someone older than you wanting to be with you is laughable.

"And I, uh—" His hand reaches to cup the back of his neck. The dude is nervous. In the entire month I've known him, I have never seen him shaken.

What the fuck is going on?

"Uh... you know how we're supposed to pretend to date?" he asks, avoiding my eyes.

I nod, holding my breath.

Oh shit, he's so repulsed by me he's trying to let me down gently.

Way to be an idiot, Hal.

"Well, I'd like for it to be real."

"It's okay, Luke. You don't have to date me. I know—" I blink. "Did you just say you want to date me for real?" My voice squeaks, and he chuckles, nodding.

"Yeah. What do you think about that?" he asks, and I suddenly feel weak in the knees.

Shit.

Stumbling to the bed, I flop down beside him, so I don't have to worry about falling over and making an idiot of myself.

"I've never kissed anyone before," I blurt out, then cover my face with a groan.

Way to keep being an idiot.

He chuckles.

"I like that I'd be your first," he whispers, and I open the fingers of my hands to peek through, taking in the seriousness on his face before dropping them into my lap.

"Really?" I ask, swallowing my nerves.

"Really. I've been fighting it for weeks," he admits, inching closer to me until our thighs are touching. When his hand cups my cheek, it sends a jolt of electricity through me.

"Me too," I admit, and he groans, searching my eyes.

"Are you agreeing to be mine, Scratch?"

I take a deep breath and nod, unable to find the words to speak right now. Not that it matters.

He closes the distance between us, softly running his lips over mine a few times before I get impatient, moving my tongue along the seam of his lips.

He lets out a groan before his mouth opens, pushing his tongue against mine as his hand moves to the back of my neck, caressing me there.

The kiss doesn't last nearly as long as I'd like it to before he pulls away, both of us breathing harder. I'm completely dazed right now.

"Damn. That was better than I expected," he whispers, and I scoff before thinking better of it. "Not what I meant. It's just never felt like that with anyone else before," he states, and I blink at him, narrowing my eyes to see if he's being sincere.

When I don't get any bad vibes, I breathe a sigh of relief.

"Well, if it helps, I didn't think it would be like that either." I shrug, trying to make light of what's happened because my nerves are high, and my heart is beating a million miles a minute.

Lukas

SHE'S AFRAID. Of what, I can't be sure, but I think it's a combination of things.

I know she can sense the guys watching her when we're out and about, even when they aren't in sight. It's like being paranoid is ingrained into her very being and it makes me want to murder the bastard chasing her.

I feel like I don't know everything yet, but I know enough to know she's innocent and needs our help. That I will die if it means keeping my girl safe.

God, she's so fragile and tiny. She has quickly become a huge part of my life. My heart.

This could make a serious mess if the FBI tools find out, or if we break up or some shit, but I don't see that happening, and I know the Chief will understand. He knows I always put the job before my own feelings, and the fact that her safety and my feelings line up, makes it an obvious choice.

There's just something about her that makes me feel settled, and that has only ever happened with my brothers before.

There's just something uniquely different about Haliee Morgan. I knew I had to make her mine, and worrying about the FBI doesn't mean we aren't telling anyone.

Actually, I already talked to her father. He wasn't necessarily happy about it, but he said he saw it happening. That she's been happier and more relaxed around me than he's seen her in years.

That statement gutted me.

I'm glad I can be a comfort for her and make her smile and relax, but I hate that she's ever had to live her life in fear to begin with.

I really need to sit down with the guys and give them more details about what's going on, but I want her permission first before I get into the grittier things. And before I can ask her, I need to make sure they stop viewing her as a threat.

It's a wire I'm walking very delicately, trying to balance everything so the full truth can come out at the right time.

"Thank you for agreeing to try this." I smile at her, and her blush is fucking adorable against her pale skin.

"You're welcome?" she asks, and I laugh, earning a chuckle from her before my phone starts ringing.

Pulling it out of my pocket, I see Mathias name and have to hold in the growl that wants to escape. He wants news on my girl and he's going to get it.

But he's not going to like that I've claimed her before he's given her the all clear.

Once they know she's mine, they will have to leave her the fuck alone.

"I'm so sorry, babe. I have to go," I sigh, pushing my phone back into my pocket after rejecting the call and shooting him a text to tell him I'm on my way.

"Work?" She smiles, and I shake my head.

"No, my brother needs me."

She nods and gives me a small smile. I haven't told her much about my life yet, but she does know about Tor, and this isn't really a lie. He may not have called, but he will be there along with everyone else.

Sometimes a little grey area is needed to navigate a minefield like this one. We're crossing a lot of supposed boundaries that were put in place to protect everyone.

"Do I ever get to meet this elusive brother?" she sasses, and I chuckle, leaning in to give her a quick kiss.

"Yeah, I think that can be arranged. Text me if you need anything, alright?" I hand her my number and she looks confused. "You're my girl now. That's my private number that I always have on me."

She beams up at me, typing the number into

her phone quickly. "Thank you, Luke." She smiles at me as I start to leave her room.

"You're welcome, Scratch." I stop, looking over my shoulder. "Text me for the fun of it too, yeah? I miss you at night." I wink before leaving with a smirk on my face.

I got the girl.

HALIEE:

Miss you already. I can't believe this is happening.

THAT's the first text I open when I get back to the house. God, she's cute as hell.

I know it's strange for me to date her when there's ten years between us, but fuck. I've never felt drawn to anyone the way I do her.

She's like this soft and sweet light in the midst of our dark world, and I just want to keep her for myself to keep her safe.

When I first saw her at the station, the immediate attraction was obvious, but I've never let myself get close to anyone except the guys before.

It's my job to protect them and this town so kids don't ever have to grow up the way they did.

Torren and the others are all eight years younger than me. If you had asked me if I was willing to take on their world of problems back then, I would have said no.

But the second I showed up to save my brother from that hell hole and make sure he never had a worry again, he refused to leave unless I took the other five with us. They had bonded in that place, and he refused to be separated from them.

I wasn't leaving my brother there so, in the end, taking them all wasn't even a question.

It was a struggle at first, getting used to so many people in my space, but it was worth it.

Aside from Dad and Torren, I had never allowed myself to be near people because I couldn't be bothered.

It didn't take long until the seven of us were completely inseparable, and as I learned their back stories, I found myself as pissed for them as I was for my own brother.

The violence and action we started by taking on their enemies was a natural progression for us. But once we hunted and destroyed their ghosts, abusers, and rapists, we still weren't sated.

We were meant for more. That's why I joined the force.

It wasn't a natural choice for me, but it did give us leads while helping me learn how to better hide evidence. It gave me knowledge and leverage, and that meant power.

Power over the rapists, pedophiles and abusers of the world.

We have one rule though. We don't make decisions alone. The next target is always agreed upon amongst us as a group. It's how we do everything.

Sighing, I take a deep breath before responding to my girl, ready to face the shitstorm from my brothers for claiming her without talking it over with them first.

LUKE:

Miss you too, Scratch. And trust me, it's happening ;).

. . .

Sliding my phone into my pocket, I get out of the truck and head into the house, readying myself for whatever they throw at me.

Haliee is innocent and beautiful. A complete goddess of light in this fucked up life we live.

I just need to make them see it.

Mathias
Chapter Six

I can tell by the way he walks into the living room that something has changed, and my insides start to crawl.

Fuck, I hate when things change. I knew the second I saw him with her that first day, that she would change everything.

I bet she doesn't even know just how much her very existence is about to wreak havoc on six other lives.

"What's up, man?" Torren asks.

He shrugs, falling onto the couch beside him and swiping an unopened beer off the table.

None of us are actually twenty-one yet, but he doesn't really stop us from drinking. After the lives we've had, I think we're entitled to a little alcohol to destress every once in a while.

"Where's Creed?" Lukas asks, and we all shrug.

We aren't supposed to go anywhere alone, but that little fucker sneaks off all the time on us. We've kind of given up on trying to stalk his dumb ass because we know there is nothing out there that's scarier than him.

He's safe.

"Fuck. If he touches her, I will personally kill him. I hope you know that." He scrubs his hand down his face before looking at each one of us with fire and determination. "That goes for any of you. Haliee is officially off fucking limits."

"Seriously?" Torren's eyebrows are lost in his hairline as he watches his brother.

"Yes. She's mine, and she's off limits. It's that simple," he growls, and Tor visibly swallows. He's never seen Lukas like this. None of us have.

Whenever one of them have sex, it's a wet pussy and nothing more. Lukas has never strayed from that path.

What makes this tiny thing so fucking different?

"She's eighteen," I point out, and his head snaps toward me.

"Your point?"

"How much do you really even know about her, Luke? We can't find shit on her. We know nothing."

He smirks at me. "I'm aware of that."

My blood boils as I realize that he's the one who made it that way. He knew we would look into her and that Witness Protection had nothing on Oliver when we decided we wanted the information.

"You son-of-a-b-itch! How are we supposed to trust you when you won't tell us anything about her?!" I bellow, trying to stay in my seat. I don't like resorting to my emotions or violence. I prefer to be the sane and rational one in our group, but I'm teetering on the edge of throttling him.

"I know everything there is to know about her background, and I'm well on my way to knowing everything about her that she's been forced to keep buried most of her life." He doesn't raise his voice, doesn't make a move to hit me. He's that solid in justifying his actions when it's a complete betrayal to the rest of us.

"That's kind of fucked up," Barren says softly, and Luke looks up and sighs.

"You wouldn't have listened to me, and she really is in danger here. I'm just trying to keep her safe and do my job."

I snort. "Is fucking her a part of your job? Or is that just a perk?"

His jaw ticks and I know I've hit a nerve. "She's not a perk, asshole. She's someone who has been through hell and is finally getting to live some semblance of a normal life. If anyone could understand that, I would think it would be the six of you."

"We need to know the truth. If this is you claiming her as your girl, it means she falls under our protection too…but we can't do that without knowing what we are up against. You say she is in real danger? Tell us why," Torren says.

He looks between us, swallowing hard as a look of defeat washes over him.

"Maybe it's best Creed isn't here for this, anyway." He sits up straighter, and we all nod. Creed is Wrath and extremely impulsive. Its best Ollie breaks the news to him. Fucking the hatred out of his system is usually the only way he can think clearly again.

"Go on," Tor encourages his brother.

"There's this Russian guy named Dimitri Koschov that's after her." What the fuck? "Apparently, her parents were a one-night stand, but Brendon, her father who goes by Brent now, stuck by her when he found out he was going to be a Dad." He takes a deep breath. "But he wanted nothing to do with her mother, and she didn't want Haliee anyway. When she was born, her mother signed over her parental rights."

"None of this is connecting yet," Corden points out, and Luke shoots him a glare.

"I'm getting there. The mother had a lot of gambling debts, and her life was on the line. Basically, she sold her little girl as a way to relieve her debt and save her own life."

I think I'm going to be sick. "She sold her? How do you mean?"

He actually physically pales and it's all I need to know, but he says it anyway. "As a little virgin sex slave to ever only belong to Dimitri."

The other guys are cursing, some of them being triggered. Aside from me, Oliver is the closest one of us to knowing that type of scenario.

His family grew up in the church and were die hard religious fanatics. They arranged marriages for all of their girls by the time they were sixteen years old, and often to older men.

Oliver was the only boy, being groomed by the priests to do horrible things to whatever woman he was going to be forced to marry. It all changed when his older sister killed herself rather than go through with what every other girl in the compound had suffered.

When she died, Oliver decided to run.

We aren't aware of everything that went down during his grooming, but we can wager some guesses, and none of them are good. The guy is as fucked up as the rest of us.

Me, I was never sold, but I was beaten to a pulp if I didn't clean and tidy everything just right and to my parents' liking.

Fuck, they started wailing on me before I was even out of diapers because I wasn't behaving in the manner to which they thought I should.

It's why no one, and I mean absolutely no one, is allowed to touch me now. Not even the guys.

"Fuck," Ollie curses from the floor and looks afraid. "We need to keep Creed away from her. If she's truly in danger, then we aren't her enemies. But he won't see it that way. He hasn't even laid eyes on her, and he's already obsessed with the thought of how he can break her," he groans. "The second Mathias said she was pretty, he was hooked. Then Corden came home blabbing about how sexy as fuck she is, and he's been like a dog with a bone ever since."

Fuck, not good.

"Where is he, Oliver?" Lukas growls, and he looks rightfully afraid.

"I don't know. He's probably out looking for her." He winces as we all start yelling, standing and getting ready to find Creed.

She's not a threat to us, so he can't touch her. If he does, he will never forgive himself.

Creed
Chapter Seven

She's so pretty. So pure. Be a shame if someone were to taint that.

Ha! Who the fuck am I kidding? It's me. The demon that should have never been let out of Hell. I'm the one that will taint her and love every second of it.

She has no fucking clue what's lurking outside her window right now. Wearing a cute little tank with kitten shorts, she seems oblivious to my presence which makes her really fucking stupid.

She should never let her guard down because you never know what demon is lurking around the corner.

I watch while she walks out her bedroom

toward the bathroom before I gently open her window. Her having a trellis outside of her window is extremely convenient.

I quietly crawl through and land in a crouch on her bedroom floor, and scoff. That was too damn easy. Lukas is doing a shit job at keeping this chick safe.

I walk over to her dresser and start shifting through the drawers when I hear the bathtub come on.

Smiling to myself, I grab a white pair of her cotton undies and pocket them, creeping out along the wall to peep through the crack in the door of the basic bathroom.

The little Doll is currently naked and stepping into the tub.

She has little, dusty rose nipples sitting perfectly in the centre of ample breasts. I feel my dick start to harden in my jeans and have to stifle a groan.

Fuck.

All that innocent, milky white skin would look so beautiful covered in blood from the cuts I make.

I'd never mark her enough to leave scars, though. Her skin is way too pretty for that.

I have to palm myself through the denim to seek some kind of relief while she's humming some bullshit tune with those headphones on, not caring a single thing about the monsters lurking in the shadows. Her content sigh makes it clear that she feels safe.

Wrong move, little Doll.

For someone that's in danger, she seems really unbothered and it's pissing me off. Lukas is watching over a fucking snake.

They don't have to worry, though. I'll scare this little lamb away from them all…after I've had my fun.

I watch her bring the loofa down her neck, journeying through the valley between her breasts and head further south to the V between her legs. A small gasp leaves her when she comes in contact with that pretty pink pussy.

Goddamn.

I flick the button on my jeans, staying as silent as possible while I watch this little porcelain Doll start playing with herself, before reaching in my pants and pulling out my hard length.

Rubbing the tip, I smear the precum down and start to jerk myself. I watch while she tosses her head back on another gasp, her fingers moving through the water, bringing her higher and higher to her peak.

I start pumping faster, using my other hand to fish out my blade from my hip. As quiet as a mouse, I flick it open and bring it down to where my dick is getting a workout over this beauty.

"Lukas!" she calls out when she tips over that mountain. I make a small nick right at the side of my cock that sends me over the edge with her.

Lukas. Now that's interesting.

I wonder what it will be like to have my name on her lips like that.

No. Fuck that. She doesn't deserve it. Seeing firsthand how she's playing my boy, I'd rather give her my calling.

Wrath.

I'll watch blood run from her pretty little neck while she's got my cock buried in throat if she ever says my name.

My phone starts to buzz in my back pocket, so I turn to make my way out. I can't resist wiping my cum under the Doll's pillow so I can watch her sleep in it tonight. Just the idea of her face being so close to my spend has me getting hard again.

I slip back out her window and shut it silently as possible before making my way back into the tree line where I was watching from earlier.

"One day you will learn how to lead, Creed. But to do

that you must learn to follow and obey. Now be a good boy and kneel by my desk..."

FUCK! I grab my head to loosen the preacher's vile fucking voice from my mind.

No, goddamn it! I can't think about that right now!

My chest heaves from the effort it takes to keep from throwing up my lungs.

Why in the hell did I have a flashback now of all times!?! Ollie better be ready when I get back, because I feel my demon clawing and roaring to come out and play.

I made sure the day I left that hell, that the motherfucking preacher was sent straight to the Devil he loved to base his sermons on.

For the path of the wicked shall face the judgement of the Lord.

Well, I'm not the Lord but I came close enough to the asshole when I slit the preacher's throat and took his head from his body.

It was the first time I killed. The first time I felt someone else's life in my control as the blood drenched my hands.

My pants were still hanging around my ankles and his grunts at my back quieted when I snatched the ceremony dagger from his desk and sank it into his neck.

I snatched my pants up, and this intense feeling of euphoria came over me as I watched the blood pour from the wound, his eyes wide and panicked as the last of his life drained away from the piece of shit.

I found out that day how hard it is to cut off a head. Between tendons and bone, it wasn't simple or quick, but the preacher always booked our sessions in length because he liked to beat and torture me, the disgusting fuck.

"Oooomph." Air rushes out of me as I slam to the ground, a body on top of me and I snap, letting the demon out to play.

Torren
Chapter Eight

He's watching her window like a creep. I just hope we got here before he did anything overly fucking stupid because Luke will kill him.

I tackle him to the ground, taking him by surprise. He's still for just a moment before he starts bucking and thrashing, trying to throw me off and no doubt kill me.

He's not himself right now, and I know that because he would have heard me coming otherwise. The only one that can usually reach him when he's like this is Ollie.

He throws himself back in a violent attempt to break free that throws us both off balance and sends us rolling farther away from the house.

"Get the fuck off me unless you want to die!" he hollers, and I have to move my hand to his mouth to shut him the fuck up. We can't be made here, not when there's cops watching her house. We also don't know who else may be watching.

"Creed! It's me, Tor! You need to calm the fuck down, asshole!" I snarl as he tries to bite my hand, but he doesn't stop.

I know how Ollie handles Creed and his demons, and I'm most definitely not willing to take his violent dick in my ass.

Now or ever for that matter, but there has to be another way.

"Creed, she's innocent. You hear me? Lukas filled us in. She's in Witness Protection to get her away from someone who is even sicker than WE had to deal with," I snarl, and his breathing is heavy as he goes deadly still.

"What did you say?" His teeth are grinding together. I'm not sure if he's pissed I mentioned our pasts, or that someone is after her.

He's too complex to figure out how his mind works, but if he's watching her right now and has already been here for a while, then his obsession has already grown.

"I said she's in danger from someone worse than what we had to go through."

He growls, nodding at me that he won't do anything stupid. It takes a few seconds for me to decide whether or not I believe him before I inevitably move.

"Who?" he asks me, his eyes as black as the night sky around us, swirling with uncertain danger.

"Some Russian guy."

"More!" he grinds out through clenched teeth, his eyes moving back to the window of her room. Or what I assume is her room.

Luke is on his way here, hoping that she's safe and doesn't need him, but needing to be sure.

"Her mother sold her innocence to pay a debt. She's supposed to belong to this Russian creep who wants her as his slave. His sex slave."

He grimaces before squinting his eyes. "Mine."

Oh, shit, he's more obsessed than normal. This is going to be delicate.

"Creed, we need to go. Luke will fill you in at home, but you definitely can't be here. WE can't be here. There are cops everywhere watching her."

He scoffs and shakes his head. "Imbeciles. Useless. Mine."

Fuck, fuck, fuck.

"Luke is coming to check on her and the security. I need to get you home to Ollie." His eyes snap to mine, and I hold my hands up. "He's not in danger, but he's worried about you. Please come home with us so we can make a plan."

He blinks, looking back to her room longingly before a dark smirk crosses his face as she shuts the lights off. I assume she's going to bed.

"Fine." He stomps off toward the street where I parked, just as Lukas pulls up.

"Un-fucking-believable. If you hurt her, I will murder you, Creed." My brother is as furious as Creed was just a few moments ago, and I know this won't end well. We need to get out of sight right now and deal with this at home.

"Lukas, not now," I plead with him. "Let's do this at home." He looks at Creed with venom before nodding.

Just as we are about to leave, her scream overtakes the night, echoing through the forest. Lukas doesn't even look at us before speeding toward her house.

"What the fuck did you do?!" I snap, pulling away before we're caught anywhere near the house. Unlike Luke, we have zero reason to be here.

His creepy-ass smile widens across his face as his eyes sparkle.

"I left my little Doll a bedtime present."

What the fuck does that even mean?! I know there's no point in asking for clarification, but fuck. With him, that could be anything.

Haliee

DON'T PANIC. *Don't panic.*

Yeah right, I'm panicking.

"WHAT THE FUCK?!!!!!!" Huh, that make me feel minutely better until Dad runs into the room.

"Haliee? Haliee!"

Shit. "I'm okay." I let him know, so he can calm down. Am I okay? Fuck no!

Who the fuck was in my room long enough to leave their jizz under my goddamn pillow?!

I shiver at the idea of Dimitri being so close while I was bathing. Could he have found me? He's never done anything like this before. Neither have his goons. I'm pretty sure he would kill them for taunting me this way when he wants me all to himself.

Fuck this. I'm never listening to music again. I knew I was getting too comfortable here.

"Sparrow, what's wrong?!" Dad grabs me by the arms, and I realize I'm crying.

Fucking, fuck! Why can't I just be happy without anyone trying to scare me?!

"M—my pillow. Dad, someone was in here while I was taking a bath."

"What?" He steps toward the bed, only taking one hand off of me before grabbing my pillow, his face draining of colour when he sees what's on it. "Get packed, Haliee. We're leaving."

I nod, whimpering and unable to move. I know we should leave. It's the only way to be safe, but I had really hoped the FBI would be able to help us.

Guess I just don't get to be happy or live a normal life.

"K," I whisper, pulling away just as someone starts running up the stairs.

Oh shit. Are they already here? Are we too late?

I run to my dresser and grab the knife I know I'm skilled with. I'm not going to go down without a fight, and I'm sure as hell not losing Dad.

"Haliee? Baby, are you okay?!" I hear Lukas

screaming from the top of the stairs, and feel a warm peace wash over me.

Maybe he will keep me safe. He's always here for me, right? Even if it was just a job at the beginning.

I don't answer him, so Dad does.

"Lukas, we're leaving," Dad tells him as Luke runs into the bedroom, his face full of fear.

"Leaving? What?" He looks between Dad and I before I drop to the ground, too emotional to hold myself up.

I'm so tired. I just want to live my life and be normal. The constant running and fighting is just too much anymore.

"Baby. Scratch, tell me what's wrong." Lukas sinks down to the ground in front of me, grabbing my chin.

I shake my head, the emotions too much to talk right this second.

"Someone broke into her room and left their cum under her pillow."

Lukas stiffens in front of me, his face turning a dark red and purple. "Package it up in this. We will run tests to see who it was and we'll increase security. From here on out, I will sleep on Haliee's floor so no one can hurt her. Running isn't going to work.

She needs a normal life." He hands Dad a pair of gloves and an evidence bag out of his pockets.

Do police just carry this shit around with them? I mean, I guess it makes sense to be prepared, but shit.

"You expect me to let my daughter's boyfriend, ten years her senior, sleep on the floor in her room?" Dad scoffs, and Lukas glares at him.

"I expect you to put your daughter's safety before your worry that we will be doing something you wouldn't approve of. I will never do anything to her that she wouldn't want, and I'm the best. No one can keep her as safe as you and I together."

Oh, that was smooth. Appealing to Dad by saying they're the only two for the job.

Dad is silent for a moment, his eyes hard on Lukas while he thinks. Lukas' hands are tightly wrapped around my arms like he's afraid I will run away.

"She deserves a normal life, Brent. You've only been here a few weeks. There's no way it was Dimitri finding you this soon. He's never been this quick before, right?"

Dad shakes his head. "No. It usually takes him four to six months."

Lukas lets out a breath. "Then let's take this in

for testing. Chances are it was just a local kid being a pervert, but we will up security by my being here full time, and we can put added locks on all the windows. Give me a chance to prove myself to you. Don't take her on the run again. Please." Lukas is practically begging Dad at this point.

He's silent for a moment before conceding.

"Fine. But if I hear anything other than talk and sleep coming from this room, I will ruin you."

Lukas nods, the tension leaving his body as Dad puts the gloves on and packs the sheet and pillowcase into the evidence bag.

Oliver
Chapter Nine

I'm pacing the floor waiting for Torren to show up with Creed in tow.

Torren took lead on this because Lukas couldn't be trusted to not kill Creed for whatever his inner demon was doing to Haliee.

Mathias is standing in the corner with foot propped up against the wall, and arms crossed over his chest looking completely at ease. To anyone else it looks like he's relaxed and peaceful, but I know he's anything but right now.

Sloth is a deadly snake getting ready to strike as soon as Creed walks in that door.

The group of us formed out of a necessity to survive. We forged the armour on our skin so thick nothing could ever penetrate it, and we made our last promise to God as innocent children that the innocent would be spared before our demons took root in our souls.

Whatever Creed has done, he will be punished for this. The problem is, will it be Creed or Wrath breaching the threshold of our home?

Fuck, my fingers are twitching restlessly with the need to steal something or fiddle with something on the computer to make this better for the guys. Or myself, either way I need to do something.

The moans coming from Corden's room drown out my musing. I sneer in disgust at Lust's way of dealing with stress. That bitch Amber and her cronies better be gone before Creed gets here.

If I know him at all, I know he will be out of control, and they will pay the price. They've never gotten along, and I can't halfway blame Creed for that. We didn't dub them the 'bitch squad' for nothing.

Just as the headboard to Corden's bed starts slamming against the wall, the front door flies open and Torren steps in.

"You need to get him out of the car and keep him chill long enough for me to run them out of here," he says, looking directly at me.

Fuck. I drop my head and ready myself for this fight. It'll end one of two ways. I'll be bloody in the face, or raw in the ass.

I make my way outside to see Creed still sitting in the car staring off into the distance.

Walking up, I gently tap the window. I don't want to startle him when he's like this. His head snaps in my direction, and he flings his door open.

Before I can process what's happening, I'm yanked into his lap, and he slams the door shut once more.

His lips crash into mine while my hands find purchase on his shoulders to steady myself. His intoxicating scent is suffocating me along with his rough lips. The firm muscles in my grip bunch in an effort to draw me closer to him.

My dick hardens almost instantly with how much he needs me right now.

I can get lost in Creed like this.

He pulls back a hair and shocks the hell out of me when his whispered "please" hits my ears.

Whatever happened today has royally fucked him up.

I crawl off his lap into the driver's seat, and reach for the button on his jeans.

This car is small as fuck, but I'll contort

however I need to just to get this man's cock in my mouth to give him some kind of peace from the raging fire his mind is putting him through.

He's holding back, too, which is a fucking first. His hands are gripping the console and door in an effort to not grab me. When his pants are undone, I drag them down his ass a bit, moaning a little when his solid length smacks his abs.

God, his dick is fucking delicious.

I waste no time diving in, taking him all the way to the back of my throat, swallowing him whole. Creed's head slams against the head rest while he unleashes a guttural sound that's half moan, half plea.

I get to work, bobbing my head and hollowing my cheeks while adding a little teeth to the mix to give him the pain he needs. It won't get him all the way there, but he's always enjoyed when I use my teeth.

Creed gets impatient and starts working his hips to get deeper down my throat, and I come alive knowing I'm able to give him everything he needs.

My oxygen levels are hanging on a by hope and prayer at this point, but what a hell of a way to die.

Just as I'm on the brink of passing the fuck out,

Creed pulls back and snatches the back of my head to draw me up for another bruising kiss.

"PLEASE, OLLIE!" He's never been submissive like this ever before. Whatever is tearing through his mind is wrecking him. I'll bring him back to himself no matter the cost to me, because even though we've never said the words aloud, I love him, and I know he loves me, too.

I drop my head back down, taking his hardness deep into my mouth. I reach behind my back and grab my hidden blade, quickly unsheathing it, moving it to his inner thigh.

Head still bobbing, I press more firmly until I see blood pooling at the tip of my blade. Creed hisses out a breath, and starts forcing his cock down my throat in a fast rhythm.

"Fuck. Fuuuucck. OLLIE, FUCK!" he shouts as his cum explodes down the back of my throat. I keep sucking until he's completely drained before I pull my head up to look at him, licking my lips to make sure I get every drop.

Sweat glistening and chest heaving, he's gorgeous.

I also know time is up on our little session when the front door opens and the bitch squad comes pouring out. They're screaming at the top of their lungs, still half naked and running for their lives.

I look back at Creed as he watches them with a sinister smile in place. This isn't going to be good at all.

"Let's get inside, yeah? We have a lot to air out." I try gently, but I already know it's too late when his eyes turn black, and he snatches up his pants.

I grab for him, only to get slammed back into the seat when he darts out the car and launches himself at Amber.

"Don't think for one second I don't know what you and your crew of bitches have been gossiping about on campus. The new girl is off limits. Period," he seethes as he grips her throat in his hand, shaking her like a rag doll.

"I don't know what the fuck you're talking about!" she shrieks in response, the others watching on in fear.

"Don't you, though? Or does 'Let's get Justin to drug her and have a good time to loosen up the stiff little virgin' not ring a bell?" Creed growls in her face.

My brows shoot up to my goddamn hairline as the colour drains from Amber's face. They were already gunning for Haliee? Cord is going to be pissed when he hears about this.

Fuck, when it rains it fucking pours, doesn't it?

"It... it was a joke! Right, guys!?! We were joking! Please let me go!" she wheezes out as Creed's grip tightens.

"Creed! Drop her. Now!" Torren booms from the front door.

I'm still sitting in the car like an asshole, not doing a damn thing to stop this because Amber's a spiteful bitch.

The moment she saw Haliee was the moment she wanted to destroy her. I know it because Amber doesn't do competition. And whatever she saw in Haliee, she took is as a threat to her existence.

She also thinks we are her own personal harem of men, even though most of us won't touch any of them, but her eyes are so set on Cord it's scary sometimes. She's going to become a problem eventually. We've always known it.

Fuck this. I get out the car to head back inside. I'm not Creed's keeper, they can deal with this shit. Right now, Greed is looking out for numero uno.

If those bitches were trying to go after Haliee, they just signed their own death warrants.

. . .

Barren

WHATEVER IS GOING ON, it's serious.

Breaking up Cord's little harem of pussy is not a smart decision, but it has to be serious if they didn't even let him get off first.

Fuck, he's going to be a miserable cunt to deal with until he gets laid again.

"Un-fucking-believable!" Cord punches the wall, and I barely flinch. I'm used to him getting pissy. That's not the weirdest part, though.

Through all of this shit, I'm feeling calmer than I normally would.

His anger usually sets me off and makes me antsy to run off the frustration. The desire to do so is still there, but it's not eating me alive.

"You need to chill out," I tell him.

He turns on me, eyes narrowed.

"Fuck that. He couldn't even give me ten seconds to cum first? I mean, they aren't the greatest pussies out there, but it's a hell of a lot better than my fist!"

"Cord, shut the fuck up and get out here! Both of you!" Mathias bellows through the door.

Why is everyone so unhinged tonight?

"You're pissed, I get it. But clearly this is something big. Get your head out of your ass and let's go."

"It better be fucking catastrophic, man," he grumbles at me before stomping out of the bedroom.

Deep breath in, deep breath out.

This bracelet may help me more than I would ever admit to anyone, but I get the feeling tonight may surpass the black beads and oils.

I should probably thank the girl for suggesting it, but honestly? I'd rather not get involved.

By the time I join them, everyone is standing around the kitchen with looks ranging from murder to irritation. Creed looks like he's going to kill Cord if Tor and Ollie would let him go.

"What are you fucking looking at me like that for, Creed?!" Cord growls, his anger matching Creed's.

I lied. I need to go for a run if this is how tonight is going to go. Creed is struggling against their hold, looking feral, and it's not good.

"If the bitch squad ever steps foot in here again, I will murder all of them before turning on you!" Creed snaps.

Whoa.

What the fuck?

Creed doesn't threaten us, not seriously. Ollie is the one who gets the brunt of his wrath, and he still gets orgasms from it. Whatever the fuck happened, it's got him in knots.

"Were they really planning that?" Ollie asks him quietly, never taking his eyes off Creed.

"Think I'd make that up?! She's my little Doll and if they hurt her, I will destroy them and laugh doing it. Not tasting their blood, though. Fuck knows the bitches would be filled with poison."

Yeah, gross. Wait… Doll?

"I'm lost." I look around to everyone. "And where is Luke?" Though, the answer is probably his girl.

Oh fuck. "Creed, what did you do?"

"Don't worry about what I did. My little Doll is safe, but his aren't," he sneers at Cord again, and I groan.

"Enough! Everyone sit the fuck down!" Mathias barks out.

Yep. Definitely going to need that workout tonight.

Mathias

. . .

This isn't going to go over well.

Lukas is beyond pissed at Creed for leaving his so called present under her pillow and having to clean up his mess, and Creed is murderous toward a bunch of disposable chicks for something they've said about his little Doll.

How did this shitstorm get so fucked up in under a few hours?

Once we're all seated, I explain what's happening.

"Lukas sent me a message. He's not going to be here for a while because he needs to keep watch on the girl." Haliee. I refuse to use her name right now because I don't want to set anyone off.

Things are getting out of hand a lot faster than I anticipated with her, but she's one to protect. An innocent.

"What do you mean he's not coming back?" Tor questions, pulling his phone out and reading what I assume is a message Luke sent him. "Fuck."

"What?" Barren is trying to keep his anxious ticks hidden, but I know him too well. He needs to get out of here before he loses it.

"Creed, fuck, man. That's worse than I

thought." He gags a little, and Creed just smiles triumphantly at him.

"Right. Creed stalked Luke's girl today. He still didn't know her story, and he left his cum under her pillow. It set her and her father off, so Lukas is playing damage control."

"You know something you aren't telling me about my Doll?" He turns to me, excitement filling him, but I know he's going to fucking snap. I give Ollie a look and he nods, leaning in to whisper the news in his ear.

I watch him go from anxious, to murderous and possessive in under a second. This is more than his need for vengeance. He really is obsessed with this girl.

We all watch as Ollie holds him still, his body straining to hold Creed together.

"No. MINE! My Doll, Ollie. Mine!"

Guess he's pissed Luke has claimed her.

"Lukas is staying with her as added protection. She's freaked out, and he was barely able to talk her father into staying."

They all turn to me. "Staying?" Barren asks, and I nod.

"They were going to run again. Worried that this Dimitri guy had escalated, so new rule. If you're going to stalk the girl, don't leave your jizz anywhere, yeah? Save Lukas from trying to get rid of the evidence."

"He's staying with my Doll?" Creed is actually pouting.

"She's his girlfriend and the Detective assigned to her. It makes sense. Oh, and he's adding extra locks to the windows so your perverted ass can't watch her naked anymore."

"Is she as hot as I imagined?" Corden looks at Creed with wide eyes.

"Hotter, brother. So creamy and untouched," he groans, adjusting his dick.

"Fuck," Cord curses.

"Can we get back on track here?" I ask, Tor and Barren nod.

"What's this about the bitch squad, Creed?" Torren asks him while he cuts his eyes to Corden.

"They're planning to have my Doll drugged and raped at a party."

Corden loses all the colour in his face, and I wince.

He's all for consensual sex, and even rough play when he joins Ollie and Creed. But rape? That's a hard limit for him any day, let alone with someone who's already as vulnerable as Haliee Morgan.

Corden
Chapter Ten

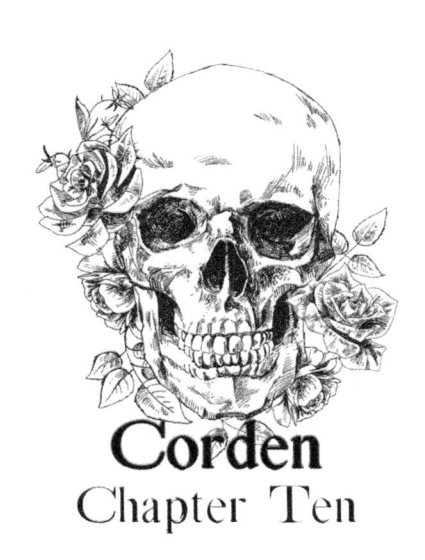

This situation went from sugar to shit in two point five seconds. My dick gets me into some fuckery, but this tops the cake.

I shoot up from my spot and head out the door, needing air to fill the lungs that have seemed to stop working on me.

"Where the fuck do you think you're going?!" Mathias yells out, but I'm too far gone in my head to reply.

My twin grabs him and whispers something in his ear. His nodding head is all I need to to see to know my twin has me covered. I can always count on Barren to be there for me, just like he can always count on me.

My pussy on supply tap has officially been cut off. How can I ever look those bitches in the eye again knowing they had some nefarious shit planned for Haliee?

It's not really the loss of said pussy that has me in stitches, it's the taking without asking. Consent is a big limit of mine.

Rape? I will gut a motherfucker with another motherfucker for even thinking about it, let alone acting on it.

That porcelain beauty will never be harmed in that manner. Now that we all know the details of her past, we can protect her our way.

Lawless, and savagely.

Amber has lost her freaking mind if she ever thinks I would support something like this. She knows we were just a fuck around deal and none of us would ever belong to a bitch like her, but she tries her best to trap us all the same.

If I didn't have a brain, I'm sure she would have found a way to get knocked up by now, but I'm not an idiot. No way will I get trapped by her or anyone else.

The first time she pulled this jealous possessive shit, I fucked her mother and let Amber walk in to see me nailing her mommy from behind.

Good times. That old lady had some good fucking moves, let me tell you.

I'm so lost in thought that I hadn't realized I'd made my way through the woods.

I hate coming into this overgrown shit because I know every bug and creepy, weird legged fuck has its beady eyes on me.

Fuck this.

I turn and start making my way back toward the house so we can start a gameplan about what we need to do to set up the protection Haliee needs.

Before I make it two steps, I feel the lightest touch of silky strings hit my face, and I lose all semblance of having my shit together.

Chopping my arms out, screeching like a bitch and ninja kicking to get this eight-legged freak and his home off me, I drop to the ground and start patting myself all over to rid of it. I fucking hate bugs.

"CORDEN! WHERE ARE YOU, BROTHER!?!" I hear Ollie yell out.

"HERE!" I squeal back like a five-year-old girl. I am a sex god, and I've been reduced to a whimpering mess on the ground. So fucking pathetic.

I manage to get the rest of the itchy shit off my face and just lay in the dirt for a minute to catch my bearings. That's when I feel the telltale signs of creepy, crawling legs working their way around my torso.

OH, HELL NO!

I rip off my shirt and dart toward the nearest tree, slamming into it. Scratching my back and front against the rough bark, I feel blood starting to drip from how hard I'm trying to get this motherfucking spider OFF me, but I don't give a shit.

I need to be sterilized, stat!

Oliver finally spots me and runs over to see what has me in a tizzy.

"Ollie, if anyone asks, I fought a goddamn bear back here. Understood?" I tell him more than ask, glaring at him as he watches me with clear amusement in his eyes. Asshole.

Holding back his laughter, he manages to wheeze out an "ok" before we turn and make our way back toward the house again.

Fuck nature.

Lukas

HALIEE IS STILL FREAKING the fuck out, and I'm going to murder Creed when I see him.

It's one thing to be a creepy fucker with anyone else, but my girl? Hell no.

The fact he saw her naked also pisses me off. That's a luxury even I haven't gotten considering we just started this relationship. There's no way I'm going to push her into anything, especially after she admitted to me being her first kiss.

Yeah, no. The long game is the only way to go with my girl.

"Hey, baby. You should try to sleep." I reach up from the floor to hold her hand, and she sighs.

"Can you sleep with me? Luke, I'm scared." Her voice is small, and I have to hold back the cold fury coursing through my veins.

Fucking Creed.

"Sure, Scratch. But your Dad might castrate me." I wink at her with a smile as I stand up and climb into bed with her. As she settles onto my chest, I feel content for the first time maybe…ever.

She's a light for me, and keeping her safe is my sole focus. Our sole focus.

My brothers won't let anything happen to her now that they know she's not a threat. We don't tolerate people threatening women and children. Add onto that, that she's my responsibility and my girl? She's finally going to be safe.

Well, safeish. Creed is a wild card and according to Torren, he's obsessed with her.

I'm going to have to keep an eye on his psychotic ass.

"Don't worry. I'll protect your precious junk," she snorts at me, and I chuckle.

"Why, thank you, Scratch. My tiny hero." I squeeze her tight, and she sighs.

"Thanks for doing this, Luke. I know this goes beyond your job."

"Haliee, look at me, baby." She moves her head until her chin is resting on my chest and looks up at me. She's so beautiful. "Sleeping in the same space as my girl is absolutely no hardship." I wink, and she rolls her eyes.

"Yeah?" she questions, and I nod.

"Yeah, baby."

"Okay. Can we watch a movie or something? I can't sleep."

I grimace. Please don't be *The Notebook* or some horrid chick flick. I'll do it for her, but damn. "Yeah, anything you want."

She gives me a sly smile before moving over me to reach for her backpack on the floor, and her ass ends up right in front of my face.

All round and curvy, and so fucking biteable. I groan, and she looks back at me with a question as my dick grows hard.

She's going to be the death of me. Holy fuck.

Moving back to the inside of the bed, she opens her laptop, hiding the screen from me as she picks a movie. What is she up to?

"So, don't laugh at me, but this is one of my all-time favourites."

She hits the space bar and sets the computer up at the end of the bed for us to watch before she snuggles into me again.

I'm just about to concede that I have to sit here for the next three hours watching some bitch ass movie when *The Boondock Saints* starts playing.

"No fucking way!" I gasp in shock, and she chuckles. "This is seriously your favourite movie?!"

She chuckles and nods. "Totally is. They're seriously badass. Anyone who kills evil assholes is epic in my book. Plus, they're so hot."

Oh, that does it. I attack her sides, tickling the hell out of her as she giggles and laughs until she's gasping for air and smiling.

"Totally hot, huh?"

She nods. "Yep, but don't worry. They've got nothing on you, babe." She winks at me. "Now shhh."

I chuckle, pulling her close and feeling content to watch the movie while holding her. If she truly feels that way, maybe she can handle the real me along with my brothers. But I'm not delusional. That's going to be a hard pill to swallow.

I just hope she doesn't try to run after.

Hailee

I'M SAFE.

I keep turning those two words over in my mind. Even laying here in Lukas' arms, I know I am, but I can't get my heart to settle.

"Tell me something you're passionate about," Lukas whispers in my ear. It's like he can sense how unsettled I am, and it should scare me, but it doesn't.

It's been a long time since I've given any thought to what I'm passionate about outside of Psychology.

I've never been able to settle in one place for too long, so that limits the hobbies department, but there is one thing...

"I like animals. Even though I've never had one before, anytime we moved on to a new place, I always found a stray that, for just a minute I could imagine having. I'd feed them and give them water, then just sit with them a while," I start to tell him. "I know that some strays can be wild animals and dangerous, but I've never come across one that didn't come straight to me. It's like they know that they can trust me." I shrug. "Sometimes, a dangerous animal is just a soul needing a light in the darkness they were thrown into."

"Same thing can be said for people, Scratch. Life deals a shit hand to some, and they have no choice but to become wild animals in order to survive," Lukas says, rubbing his hand up and down my arm.

I mull over that for a minute. What he's saying is very true. We become whatever we need to be in order to survive.

He starts tracing circles on my arm. Adjusting

himself behind me, he moves and I can feel the huge asset he's clearly bringing to the table.

Damn. I may be a virgin, but that's a nice sized flashlight he's packing in those pants.

I shouldn't egg him on. Really, I shouldn't.

Dad is in the other room and has already threatened to make him a literal dickless wonder, but I can't help myself.

I arch my back so subtly that it seems I'm readjusting, but I'm getting hot here. I play with toys and shit, but for once, I want to feel what it would be like to be with someone else.

Lukas' hand freezes on my arm.

"You're playing with fire, Scratch. Don't make it burn tonight," Lukas breathes in my ear.

Well, damn. I thought I had been sneakier than that.

"What if I don't want to stop? What if I'd finally like to choose for myself?" I have no idea where I find the courage to say that, but after living my life on the run and today's incident, I need to do something that's just for me. And tonight, I want to be reckless with my hot as fuck boyfriend.

"You're lost in your head, babe. Let's just watch the movie. I don't want us doing anything that you will regret later. Please. I'm trying to be a gentleman." Lukas starts trying to play hero as always.

"I'd never reject you, Lukas. For the first time in my life, you're the best thing that's happened to me," I say, turning my head to look him in the eye.

He's holding himself as still as a statue. I don't even think he's breathing at this point.

"Fuck it. I'm not a goddamn saint," he growls out before he swoops in and starts devouring my mouth.

Oh. My. Shit.

His tongue tangles with mine as his hand moves behind my neck to get me closer somehow. Before it gets any heavier, he rips his head back, breathing hard.

"I won't take you like I want tonight. But I'll give you what you need to take the edge off. You tell me at any moment if you feel uncomfortable or uncertain, and this stop. Understand?" He all but demands.

I'm dazed and drunk on his kiss, so I nod my head in response.

"Words, Scratch. I need those words, or I won't go any further," he tells me.

I barely get "yes" whispered before he swoops back in and takes my mouth with his.

He moves his fingers down my neck, over my chest to cup my breast. Using two fingers, he gently pinches my nipple before rolling it between them.

I whimper into his mouth, pushing up to get closer while rubbing my thighs together to try and relieve the tension building from such a simple act.

"You're going to need to stay as quiet as possible, babe. I adore you, but I also fancy keeping my dick attached to me," Lukas whispers.

He moves to the other nipple and give it the same treatment but with a little more pressure this time.

"Please," I breathe out.

He chuckles while he moves his hand over my belly and cups me through my thin sleep shorts.

"Tell me, Scratch. Are you soaking wet for me right now? If I pull those panties aside, will I find you dripping for me?" Lukas whispers in my ear.

"Yes," I quietly moan.

"Does this pretty pink pussy need something to fill it? When you touch yourself, is it me you think of?" Lukas whispers, nipping my ear this time.

"Yes," I moan again, a little louder than before.

"Show me. Show me how you touch yourself when you think of me," Lukas demands.

I quickly make work of shedding my shorts and

panties before I reach down and run my fingers over my clit, arching my back when I feel that bundle of nerves light up.

"Can I touch myself while I watch you, baby? My cock could probably cut granite at this point, but if you're not ready for that, tell me and I can go have a shower," Lukas croaks, looking like he's in pain.

"Please. I want to see you too." I'm almost desperate to see him as well.

He rips open the button of his pants and pulls them down his ass a bit. Commando. Naughty boy.

I watch his length bob out, and holy shit is it a sight to see.

Thick, round, and curved slightly to the left. I'd never be able to fully close my hand around it that's for sure.

He locks his eyes on me and spits in his hand, reaching down to grabs ahold of his cock. Massaging up and down as he twists his fist, groaning in pleasure.

I feel a flood of wetness running down my centre from watching such an erotic sight up close and personal.

"Keep going, baby. Get me off by getting yourself off. I've never seen anything so fucking gorgeous in my life. Rub that pussy for me," he groans out while continuing his up, down, and around motion.

I cannot look away from him.

He's wrong. He's the gorgeous one. I start strumming my fingers across my clit a little faster, and slide two fingers from my other hand inside myself to hit that perfect rhythm.

This is the hottest thing I've ever done.

I feel the signs of my pending orgasm starting to reach a crescendo just as Lukas moves his hand faster.

"Fuck, Scratch. Give it to me. Let me see your beautiful face as you cum all over your hand, baby," Lukas whispers desperately.

My eyes start rolling into the back of my head as I hit that peak and crash over as the waves of pleasure hit me.

"Yes, baby. Fuck, yes, that's it. So perfect. So damn beautiful," Lukas chants as he finds his own release as well.

I turn my head just in time to see his cum hit his abs as he groans through his orgasm.

Breathing heavily, we lay on the bed for a minute to catch our breath, then bursting into a fit of giggle out of nowhere, and it's the perfect way to bathe in the afterglow of this experience.

Sure, Lukas didn't touch me or get me off, but for once I had control over what happened, and he made sure of it.

"Sparrow? Are you two okay in there? Do I need to sharpen my knife already?" Dad asks, knocking on the door.

The blood drains from Lukas's face as he whispers out, "I guess that was the farewell party for my dick, then."

I burst into laughter at the sad look on his face before telling Dad everything is fine.

Torren
Chapter Eleven

I'm sitting here in a daze because this is my circus, and these assholes are my monkeys.

It's been a week since Creed pulled his bullshit with Hailee, and damn this motherfucker can hold a grudge.

I watch as Corden picks Creed up, and body slamming him back to the floor.

"Ouch. I've got ten bucks for a head injury. Anyone want to raise that broken wrist to fifty?" Ollie says, watching the match with rapt attention.

"I'll match it," Mathias says from his spot in the corner, as always.

"Fuck that, I'll raise it," Barren laughs out as Corden takes another left cut to his jawline.

I shake my head and sit back.

"I'm throwing a hundred down that Creed knocks him out in the next five minutes," I state with absolute certainty.

Ollie whistles low while writing down my bet. The ever-greedy bookie.

Corden manages to break the neck hold Creed put him in and takes a shot at his temple, but Creed just laughs like the psychotic motherfucker he is.

"How'd that bitch's loose-ass pussy feel, huh? Like saggy flap jacks that were reheated from the day before, I bet," Creed taunts.

"Pussy is pussy, and I'm not a picky eater! You fucking know this!" Corden fires back.

"Got to give the bitch one thing. She'd probably be able to suck a golf ball through a water hose with the number of dicks that have plowed down her throat," Creed taunts further.

"Not as good as Ollie does." Corden smirks, pulling a low blow.

Creed roars out as we all jump up to intercept him.

Two things you don't ever fuck with Creed about. His knives, and Ollie.

I'm guessing it's three now that he won't let this Haliee thing go.

We reach Creed right as his fist connects with Corden's cheek and before we can catch him, he drops to the ground like a sack of shit. Knocked out cold.

"Fuck," Mathias mutters before going over to bitch slap Cord until he's awake again, moaning in pain. "Enough of the bitch fighting. We have someone to pay a visit to."

That gets our attention.

We're all so worked up over Haliee and this other shit with Amber and her bitch squad, that killing is going to be a nice reprieve.

"Well, what are we waiting for, then? Lead the way." I clap my hands together as Creed's mood turns bright.

Mathias

. . .

So. Fucking. Angry.

Every punch to Todd's face is another lash of anger pouring out of me over the upheaval our family is going through.

Luke hasn't been home in almost a week because he's guarding Haliee with added vigour from Creed's little stunt.

Creed is about to lose his mind if he doesn't get eyes back on her soon.

Fuck, every one of us is starting to lose our minds knowing she's in danger.

Me? I'm keeping an eye on every corner of town day in and day out, ready to take out anyone who seems intent on harming her. Haven't come across any yet, but if this Dimitri guy has been after her for this long, he's not going to give up.

The only creep that seems to be new in our quiet little town is that FBI agent. Something about him just feels off, and my gut is never wrong. But I haven't found anything on him yet.

"Can I play with him now?" Creed whines behind me as I try to catch my breath. Todd's face is bleeding and swollen, so I step back and nod.

Creed is the one who gets the bloodiest and brings them to a slow and painful death.

He needs to be the one to end it. He needs that

release of blood, and being able to watch the life drain from their beaten and tortured bodies.

We don't fuck with that.

"You had to force your own son didn't you, Todd?" Creed walks around him, his voice a deep timber. "He's eight-years-old, you sick fuck!"

The guy whimpers, but keeps his head down. Just because he's from the next town over doesn't mean he's never heard of us.

It seems that they aren't deterred. Getting their dick wet and causing children pain and mental damage is their only thought while it's happening.

I can't even tell you how many sick and twisted fucks we've rid this world of.

Between Porterville and the surrounding small towns, even a couple of big cities, we never seem to be short on scum to destroy.

You'd think they would learn.

"Please. Please, my son is fine!" the guy whimpers, and Creed's face turns thunderous.

"Is he? Hmm. Help me string him up naked, boys."

Oh, that's not going to be good.

. . .

By the time we have him stripped and hanging from a chain, he's pissed himself from fear. Just once, I'd like them to not do that. It's fucking gross.

"Here's the bag." Corden tosses a gym sized bag at Creed who's beaming from ear to ear like the psychotic serial killer he is.

We all are.

"Thanks, bro."

Cord chuckles and shrugs before coming to stand next to me. "This is going to get ugly," he mutters, and I nod. Ugly and bloody, and it's the perfect revenge before he dies.

"You're lucky my heart and dick belong to someone else." He looks thoughtful for a moment. "Two people, actually."

Lovely.

Ollie sucks in a breath on the other side of me and I look over at him, trying to decide if he's upset about Haliee taking some of Creed's attention, but all I see is love and affection for the psychotic fuck.

"I—I, what do you want?" Todd screams, shaking the chains he's hanging from in a pointless attempt to escape. He's not going anywhere.

"Me?" Creed opens the bag, making a show of pulling out all of the sex toys and torture devices he uses as his arsenal. "I'd like grown men and women to stop fucking with children. Stop raping them and beating them for their own sexual enjoyment." He pulls out a giant tentacle looking thing that has a huge bulb in the middle and I wince. That's going to fucking hurt.

"I didn't!" He screams.

Creed laughs, grabbing the dildo along with his hammer and nails.

"You did, Todd. You should confess your sins before you go to Hell. Because that's exactly where perverted fucks like you go." He shrugs, hammering over a dozen nails into the dildo until they're only sticking out about a quarter of an inch,. Knowing they won't budge, he smiles.

"God, no. Please, no!" Todd screams at the top of his lungs when he sees the instrument in Creed's hand.

"God, YES!" Creed picks up a bottle of lube and looks Todd dead in the eyes. "Don't think this is to help you. I'm just using enough for me to get the nails past your hole while it tears you end from end."

I actually have to hold back the gag when Creed walks behind him, squirting the lube and ramming it into Todd's ass. His screams of pain are shrill and loud as Creed pulls back just to shove the torture device into his ass further with each thrust.

As Todd's body jerks with every movement, the blood starts pouring out of him. A few more screams leave his mouth before he passes out.

"Stop," I say, loud enough for Creed to hear.

He stops and pouts at me.

Looking to Barren, I nod. "Get the smelling salts. His son didn't get to sleep through the pain, and neither will this bastard," I growl, and Creed cackles.

Ollie looks at me with wide eyes. "You're not usually this involved, Matt."

I nod. "I'm pissed off. You guys aren't the only ones who worry about this shit, but Haliee? She's special to our group. It means we all take part in feeling her fear and swearing to get revenge. I need to work it off somehow."

He just nods and looks back to Creed and Barren. "Fair enough. Have you seen her up close? More than that first time, I mean."

I think Ollie is the only one of us that hasn't seen her up close and in person yet.

I nod. "Yeah, a few times."

He sighs. "I figured. Is she as beautiful as they all seem to think?"

I swallow. Fuck. I'm not good with attraction to anyone.

I've never wanted or desired to be touched by another human, and attraction was never on my radar. But she's different. She seems so pure and full of light.

I'm not sure if I'm attracted to her, but I know she's different.

"She's an angel." It's the only way I know how to describe her.

Hell, I've been trying to come up with the perfect peacewarming gift. Something to make her feel better after Creed's fuck up scared her, and I have just the thing.

As soon as we're done with this sick fuck and dispose of his body, I'm going kitten shopping.

That's bound to cheer her up. Lukas mentioned she liked animals.

I spend the rest of the evening smiling like a moron to the sounds of Creed's torture and Todd's screams until he bleeds to death. His ass torn to shreds and his dick is split in two.

Time to get to the cleanup.

Hailee
Chapter Twelve

I still can't believe I got myself off in front of Lukas!

I mean, yeah, he's my boyfriend, but hello! I went from being a virgin who had never been kissed, to jointly getting myself off in front of him like some sort of voyeur.

Damn, was it hot, though.

Oh god, his dick is seriously gorgeous, too!

I've seen enough porn to know he's way above average and not even close to the toys I use. Can't exactly have anything that isn't pocket sized and easily hidden when Eagle Dad is around.

When I was sixteen, we were living in a city for

a few months, and one of my neighbours was a 'spicy accountant' if you get my drift. anyway, when we got to talking and she had found out I was a virgin, I found myself with a brand-new bullet vibrator, and wise advice.

"Honey, men these days don't give a flying fuck about getting women off. Best to learn what you like on your own, so you're never disappointed!"

I'm not sure I actually agree with her, but I wasn't going to pass up on a free sex toy. I was sixteen and horny as fuck.

Would you have turned it down? Didn't think so.

"You're lost in your head there, Scratch," Luke whispers beside me, and I jump slightly. I had totally zoned out in the middle of class which is so unlike me.

Apparently, sexy things with my new hot-as-fuck cop boyfriend is distracting.

"Shit! Sorry," I wince, and he chuckles quietly.

"Considering those perky little nipples of yours could cut glass, I'm not complaining about where your mind was at." He winks at me, smiling before turning back to the teacher so he doesn't draw attention to the blush I'm sporting. And I am sporting a wicked one right now.

Fuck, it's way too hot in here!

Damn him for being so astute to my moods!

"You look like a desperate slut right now," one of the bitch squad members says from the row behind me.

My cheeks flame, and my humiliation is almost instant.

Lukas turns and sends her a death glare, but the damage is done. I've never in my life been on the receiving end of bullies, and these last few weeks have been difficult because of these pretentious bitches.

"Weren't you literally just getting railed by two football players behind the Science Hall for a hit of coke, Liza? If you're going to call someone a slut, make sure you add your name to the top of that list," Kristen pops off from the row in front of me.

The class breaks out in giggles and gossip almost immediately while the professor tries to regain order.

I watch as Kristen arches her eyebrow and waits for Liza to refute her. Liza is beet red from head to toe with her mouth closed up tight. Bet it wasn't when she was being railed.

Jealous bitch.

I can't help the pride that fills my chest. That's my best friend right there.

"Since it's obvious that we can't control ourselves past high school puberty, you are all excused for the day," the professor says as he finally loses his last bit of patience with us.

I start packing my things away as Lukas waits on me. Before I have a chance to even grab my backpack and sling it over my shoulder, Agent Daniels walks into the classroom like he's on a mission.

Lukas rears his head back, shocked by his appearance.

"Lukas, Haliee. Can I have a quick word, please?" Agent Daniels states more than asks, while looking pointedly at the professor to leave the room.

When the professor leaves, Lukas and I head to the front of the room before my man snaps.

"Have you lost your Goddamned mind! This is an undercover operation, and you are jeopardizing it by coming in here like this, you son-of-a-bitch!" he snarls, yanking the agent by his tie.

I'm completely stunned by the show of force, and remain frozen where I stand. I've never seen him like this before. It's kinda hot.

"I wouldn't be here if it weren't important... detective. You'd do well to remember who has the authority here. I hope you're not aiming to lose your job today," Agent Daniels hisses.

Lukas instantly releases him and takes a few steps back. Breathing deep to regain some composure.

"Then talk and get lost. I refuse to let you put her at risk."

Agent Daniels' eyes narrow. "That's exactly why I'm here. Did you think I wouldn't find out that you crossed the line and started dating your assignment?" he snaps, and my heart actually hurts. I know I started out as an assignment to him, but being reduced to a job is just fucking painful.

"Her father and the Chief are aware of our relationship. It has no bearing on how I perform my job." Lukas is practically vibrating, and I reach for his hand, squeezing it in mine until I notice him calming down some.

"I don't care. This is my operation, and I have superiors to answer to. I won't have you compromising her safety to get your rocks off."

Oh, hell no! "Enough! Lukas has done nothing BUT keep me safe. For the first time in my life, I actually have a friend and feel somewhat normal. You don't get to dictate who I do and do not see."

He glares at me while Luke looks smug, and I fight to not roll my eyes. Typical fucking men. "I beg to differ, Miss Morgan," he practically spits out and I laugh, trying to diffuse Lukas' anger some.

"You can say it's your job all you want, but I don't see your ass on the line protecting me. He risks his life every day to try and keep Dad and I safe from Dimitri, while you hide away in some office somewhere. Therefore, this doesn't concern you. It's not like we hid it, and we were going to fake a relationship, anyway."

He scoffs. "Yes, fake it," he practically growls, and Luke pulls me back behind him a bit. It's a protective move that warms my heart.

"Do you really think she would have been comfortable hugging, kissing, and getting comfortable with a complete stranger for the public eye? If anything, this makes it more real while putting HER needs first."

Daniels shakes his head. "It's dangerous and stupid, and goes against protocol. You aren't supposed to date someone you're protecting! You can't keep a clear head in a relationship."

Lukas scoffs at the same time I snort, which just pisses Daniels off further, but Luke doesn't let him get a word in.

"If you think that, then you've never cared for someone you're with, because I can guarantee you that Haliee's safety IS my number one priority."

Daniels' face is turning red as he looks between us, but he doesn't say a word, so I do.

"Anything else, Agent Daniels?" I ask.

He narrows his eyes at me before growling and storming out of the room. It's only my second time seeing him face to face, but I really don't like him. I can't exactly put my finger on why, but his charming personality isn't doing him any fucking favours.

"Luke?"

He turns to me, pulling me into a hug. "It's alright, Scratch. I've got you, baby." He's trying to comfort me, and I appreciate it, but this day has just been shit all around. I just want to go home.

"I don't trust him," I tell him the same thing I told Dad, and he sighs.

"Me neither, baby. Me neither."

Between being called a slut by the bitch squad, and Agent Daniels storming in here completely against protocol, I'm done with today. I just want to go home and pretend the outside world doesn't exist for a little while.

Mathias

WHAT THE FUCK am I thinking!?! I've repeated this sentence a million times in the last two hours since driving to the city and picking up Haliee's gift.

Of course, Ollie had to tag along because the caretaker of this group of demonic bastards was the best to handle this job.

His words not mine.

He knows what I got Haliee, just not what it looks like.

Ollie of course wanted to one up me by picking up a black rose to give her.

"So, aren't black roses supposed to symbolize death and hatred and such. Why black?" I ask, genuinely curious.

"Why, yes, Matty boy, they are, but they also symbolize obsession," Ollie replies with a twisted smile.

I run a hand down my face, keeping the other hand on the wheel. I glance in the rear-view mirror at the cardboard box in the back seat again.

The little fucker hasn't stopped meowing since I picked it up, and it's more than a little annoying.

"I can't take this anymore. I'm going in," Ollie says, twisting in his seat.

"Ollie, don't!" But I'm too late. Ollie lifts the lid to the box and his sharp intake of breath is all I need to know that this might not have been the greatest decision I've ever made on my part.

"What. The fuck… is this thing!?!" Ollie all but shouts as the cat hisses at him.

The little motherfucker looks like it slammed its face into a wall going at the speed of Mach-holy-fuck. Its eyes are as big as saucers, and its little tongue is hanging out its mouth. The thing is all white except a little orange patch on its head. Its legs also seem too short for its body, making him look even more fucking weird.

A munchkin kitty is what the lady at the store called it. No clue if it's a boy or a girl because I didn't give a damn to ask or check the bits. Probably should have, but I'm sure Haliee is a smart enough girl to figure it out.

"This has got to be the ugliest fucking thing I've ever seen in my entire life. And that's saying something considering the house call we made last week to that douche bag with the horse ass fetish going on," Ollie says, easing back into his seat.

"Shut the fuck up, Ollie. Hundred bucks says Haliee does that whole 'Aww, gosh you're adorable!' thing and hugs it between her tits," I fire back.

"When the fuck did you become so sentimental?" Ollie asks with a shit eating grin on his face.

"I'm going to punch you in the balls, Ollie. Fair warning," I say, clenching my teeth and gripping the steering wheel as tightly as I can. I don't actually want to punch him in the nuts…at least not until we're closer to home. He can be a whiny bitch sometimes.

"That's ok. Creed will just suck them in his mouth later and make them feel all better," Ollie replies with a wistful sigh.

We pull up to Haliee's cabin and get out. Setting

up the box with the rose on top, we high tail it back to my car.

Driving back down the road a ways, we find a spot to park where the car won't be noticed, and head back to enjoy the show when they turn up.

Just as we get settled, Lukas drives up with Haliee in tow.

I see Lukas narrow his eyes on the gifts, telling Haliee to hang back for a second. He approaches the box and toes it with his boot, knocking the lid off along with the rose.

The cat pops up, and Haliee all but rushes Lukas in a bid to grab it first.

"Oh, my god. This has got to be the ugliest thing I've ever seen," Haliee says, picking it up and examining it.

I feel Ollie's smug-ass eyes on me, and it makes me want to dick punch him that much more. This was a stupid fucking idea.

"BUT IM TOTALLY KEEPING YOU! Like, she's so ugly she's cute! Lukas look!" Haliee shines a megawatt smile while holding the cat up to Lukas.

I see his features soften and turn to Ollie with my own smug grin in place. He flips me off, but doesn't take his eyes away from her. This is the first time he's ever seen her before. She's intoxicating.

"I'm naming you, Hope. Welcome home, kitty," Haliee tells the fur ball while nuzzling its head.

"She's an Angel," Ollie whispers.

I can only nod. I judged her so harshly at first, and I was so damn wrong.

Lukas
Chapter Thirteen

Brothers.

I can't even be mad at them for leaving the ugliest fucking cat I've ever seen on her doorstep, because it made her smile.

My money is on Mathias being the one behind that fugly thing. Everyone else would have just seen the ugly and moved past it, but Mathias? He's a lot like my girl with being able to see past the surface.

She's so fucking happy about the thing that Brent didn't even argue about her keeping it.

Anything making her that happy is worth it.

Which brings me to why I'm sitting down here alone with my girl's father, instead of snuggling up to her and Hope.

Fuck, that crushed my heart when she named it that. As if, for the first time in her life, this furry thing gave her the chance to believe she can have a better life.

"What's on your mind, Lukas?" Brent breaks the silence, and I sigh.

"Agent Daniels came to visit Haliee and I during one of her classes. I don't trust the guy."

He curses and sits up straighter in the kitchen chair. "Is he trying to get her killed?!" he growls, and I shrug because I had the same question myself.

"I don't know what's happening with him, but I don't get good vibes from the guy. Something is just off. He came to yell at us about protocol and threatened to get me kicked off her case because we're dating."

His eyes turn dark. "Over my dead fucking body. You're the one thing giving my little Sparrow life right now. No fucking way are you going anywhere."

I snort. "Even if he fired me, I wouldn't leave her side. Nothing would change. Look, Brent there's a lot about me you don't know, and I don't really know how to bring it up. But I promise you, Haliee is one hundred percent safe as long as she's with me."

His eyes narrow as he looks me up and down. "You're not as on the level as you seem, are you kid?"

I take a deep breath and blow it out. "Would that be a problem?"

He's silent for a moment as he thinks about it before shaking his head. "Not as long as she's the priority, and she's safe and never in danger from anything you do."

I shake my head, giving him a smirk. "She's never been safer. The only thing my brothers and I do is take out the trash. If you catch my drift."

He gives me a smirk of his own before nodding. "Is she aware?"

I grimace. "Not yet. I'm trying to ease her into it. I mean, knowing she wholeheartedly believes in what the *Boondock Saints* do gives me hope."

He barks out a laugh and shakes his head with a smile. "I doubt she will find issue with it. Her life has been anything but normal. I thought you only had one brother?"

"I have one biological brother. There's a lot of back story that isn't mine to tell, but Torren met them when they were in a group home together, and they became close. Ride or die essentially, so when I went to get my brother out of there, they came too. We've been on a mission to take out the trash ever since, starting with their pasts."

His face gets dark. "They won't harm her?"

I scoff. "No. They see her as family. An innocent. She is one hundred percent safe regardless of what Daniels is up to. At least two of them are watching her and I at all times."

He nods in acceptance before leaning back in his chair. "Has she met them yet?"

"She's met a couple of them, and she's sensed the others watching. I'm planning on introducing her to them at the Halloween party."

He grunts. "Sure that's safe?"

I can feel the dark and creepy smile on my face. At least her Dad knows what he's getting into with me by her side.

"We're all going to be there. It's the safest place she could ever be."

Convincing Brent to let Haliee go to tomorrow night's Halloween party was easier than I thought it would be, given everything they've been through.

It actually means a lot that he trusts me with her safety, and I won't let him down. She's the first woman I've ever cared about and it's still weird for me to wrap my head around, but all it means is that I will protect her with everything I have.

"Hey, you were gone a while." She looks up at me as I walk in and close the bedroom door. Hope is sitting on her lap, purring louder than a fucking diesel engine, and I smirk at the ugly fluffball.

"Had to talk to your Dad about our date tomorrow night." Her eyes widen comically, and she moves Hope off her lap before getting off the bed.

"Date?!" she squeals and I chuckle, pulling her into my arms.

"Yeah, baby. We're going to a Halloween party tomorrow night." She bites her lip and looks at me.

"Will that be okay?" she questions.

I think she's referring to Amber and the bitch squad, but she shouldn't worry. According to Mathias, Creed more than took care of that bitch.

"Yeah, Scratch. Torren and the rest of the guys

will be there. You are perfectly safe with all of us watching out for you."

She smiles, rolling her eyes. "Your twin friends still look at me like they want to kill me."

I snort. "Nah. Corden wants to fuck you." I let out a little growl. "And Barren just has the weight of the world on his shoulders. They approve of you, I promise."

She nods and stands on her toes to kiss me. "Okay, but, Luke?" she whispers, and I pull my head back.

"Yeah, Scratch?"

"I'm horny."

I groan, pulling her hard against me, taking her with my lips and lifting her ass until her legs wrap around my hips. Her pussy is right against my growing dick where it's meant to be.

She has that magic about her. She gets me hard so fucking fast it's almost unbelievable.

I move us until her back is against the far wall by the window, before pulling back to look into her eyes. Her breathing is shallow and rapid, making me smirk.

"You're horny, baby?" She nods. "Would you like me to touch you and make you feel all better?"

She groans and moves in to bite my lower lip.

"Please," she whines, and I grind my cock against her, making her moan.

"Shh, baby. You have to be quiet. Can you do that?" I ask against her neck, and she nods.

Reaching between us, I pull her midi skirt up, cursing at how drenched she is already.

Whoever designed the warmer thigh-high stockings for Fall was a fucking genius. I never want to see her in anything but skirts if I get to touch her like this.

"Lukas," she whimpers against my mouth, and I push her panties aside before looking into her eyes, seeking permission. The second she nods, my fingers find her slick folds, running through them, and I have to bite down on her shoulder to muffle my groan.

"God, you're so wet for me, baby." I run my fingers through her lips a couple more times, swirling them around her clit, before pushing down slightly. She jolts in my arms, practically screaming in surprise and we can't have that.

Moving my hand away from her tight little pussy, I roll her shirt up past her breasts and kiss her hard before shoving the rolled-up shirt into her mouth. Her eyes narrow at me, and I lean over, kissing below her ear before nipping her neck, making her moan.

"You can't be quiet, baby. And with your Dad still awake, this is going to be hot, hard, and fast. Think you can handle that?" She moans again, nodding her head vigorously, and I chuckle. "Good girl."

Moving my hand back to her core, I push her panties to the side again before rubbing her clit. I move lower, pushing one finger into her tight little entrance and almost cum in my pants.

"Fuck, baby. So damn tight," I grind out, my hips jerking forward of their own volition.

"Mmgnhph," she muffles through her shirt, and I chuckle. Using my other hand so the wall takes her weight, I reach up and pull it out of her mouth to let her speak.

"Rub yourself against me. I want to feel you, Luke."

She's trying to kill me. "You sure, baby?"

She nods, swallowing. "Yes. Just don't…I'm not ready for—" I nod in understanding, kissing her beautiful mouth.

"No sex."

She nods and smiles at me before I lift the shirt back into her mouth.

Reaching between us, I undo my jeans, pulling the zipper down before taking my aching dick in my hand and groan at how hard I am for my girl.

Pumping myself a few times, I move it between us until the tip touches her wet panties, and hiss out in pleasure.

Letting go of my dick, I quickly rip her panties away so I can feel her softness, and she groans at the act, making me smirk.

"Sorry if those were a pair of your favourites," I say, before winking and moving both my hands to cup her ass before she slides down the wall on me.

With both hands gripped on her ass, I make quick work of getting my dick right where it belongs, and have to bite down on my tongue to stop the moan of pleasure that wants to escape.

"Fucking perfection. So wet and hot for me. God, baby, you were meant to be mine," I groan into her neck as my hips start to move, my cock sliding between her lower lips, and I know I won't last long.

It's all too much for her. I feel the telling signs as her tight little pussy flutters against my cock, and her back arches off the wall. Her orgasm hits her like a freight train as she lets out a muffled scream around her shirt.

I can feel the tingling at the base of my spine as I push between her lips a few more times, cumming hard and expelling all over her sweet cunt. I watch her closely as she rides out the waves of pleasure with me.

She's so damn beautiful. I'd happily spend the rest of my days worshipping her to keep that look on her face.

She finally sags against the wall and blinks up at me sleepily. I chuckle a little as pride swells bigger than my dick was a second ago, knowing I did this.

"Let's get you cleaned up and in the bed, Scratch. I'll cuddle you while we watch *Boondocks Saints 2*, hmm?" I tell her, already carrying her to bed and laying her flat, pulling the shirts from her mouth.

This girl has my heart in a damn vise. I may not be the all-consuming hero she believes me to be, but I do know one thing. I'd stay with her even in the shadows to keep her safe for the rest of my days.

Haliee

THE PROFESSOR finally wraps up his lecture for today, and I breathe out a sigh of relief.

I'm normally all for the lessons, but today he was just putting me to sleep. The class starts packing their things, and I catch Corden from the corner of my eye looking up and smiling in my direction.

I go to pick up my backpack when something slams my shoulder, knocking my bag and belongings to the floor.

"Oh, no, sorry! I'm so clumsy in these heels!" Amber sasses as Lukas pulls me away from her.

I roll my eyes and don't acknowledge her.

After all, the quickest way to shut down a bully is to ignore them.

Luke and I both bend down to pick up my shit so we can get out of here.

When I reach for my notebook, another big hand lands on top of it, picking it up and passing it to me.

"Sorry Amber's such a bitch. Here you go,"

Corden says, handing me my notebook with an easy smile while his brother watches on in silence. It's pretty easy to tell them apart because their mannerisms are so different…even if they do look identical.

I smile gently back at him while Luke glares.

I shake my head at him as we leave the classroom, heading down the hall.

"Shit! Lukas, I need to run to the car and grab my English book," I say, patting my pockets in search of my phone.

"Dammit, I think I dropped my phone in there."

"Go run and grab your phone. I'll get your book. I saw the professor head back toward the class, so the room should be open," Lukas says, giving my head a quick kiss and taking off for the car.

I spin and race back toward the empty classroom when my skin prickles. Someone is watching me.

Geez, Haliee. Get your shit together. No one is following you, so stop being so paranoid!

I try and talk some sense into myself as I enter the empty classroom. I know Luke is probably anxious about us being separated, but it's only a few minutes. Everything will be fine.

Shit.

I'm letting my guard down too much since we've been here. I've never once left my phone anywhere, knowing it could mean the difference between life and death if Dimitri came for me.

The door closes softly behind me before I hear a click. Freezing in place, I wait with bated breath.

This is it. He's been watching me, and I gave him the perfect opportunity to take me because I was dumb enough to let my guard down.

"Such a pretty Doll," I hear an unfamiliar voice whisper behind me. "I wondered if I would ever get you alone. Your guard dog really doesn't like to leave your side."

The stranger moves in behind me, his chest against my back. The feeling of his breath on my neck makes me nauseous, but I hold it back. I stay completely still and work out how to get my knife out from the back of my bra without him noticing.

"Who are you?"

He cackles darkly as he moves against me, pushing me until I'm against the white board at the front of the class before he turns me, slamming my back into it. "Hmm...I'm not sure you deserve my real name yet, Doll, so how about we go with Wrath?"

I blink at him, furrowing my brows as I try to figure him out. "Wrath? What kind of a name is that?" I taunt before I can shut the fuck up, and his eyes gleam with danger as I smart off at him.

"It's my embodiment, my inner demon. I'm sure you've heard of us by now. The Deadly Seven?" He watches my face for a reaction, but I lock that shit down.

Fuck. Are they actually real? I thought the Deadly Seven were just a myth the town believes in to keep everyone on the straight and narrow. Kristen had mentioned them to me at some point shortly after we first met, but I didn't believe her.

"Wrath is a stupid name."

Shut the fuck up, Haliee! You're supposed to be disarming him, not pissing him off!

To my surprise, he tosses his head back, laughing like a maniac.

"Oh, Doll, I like you. You're going to be such a pretty little toy to fuck."

I swallow, nerves starting to take over me.

I've done a lot of things with Lukas in the heat of the moment, but we still haven't crossed that line. I'm still completely a virgin in that regard, and now this freak is threatening to rape me?

His eyes sparkle with delight as he takes in the terror I can't quite hide.

His hands travel down my neck before cupping my breasts and groaning.

"You feel good." He tweaks my nipples roughly between his fingers, and I let out a whimper of pain mixed with pleasure.

What the fuck is wrong with me?!

"Don't, please," I plead, trying to make him stop.

"So pretty when you beg. I told him you'd be the perfect toy, and I can't wait to see you bleed all over my dick." He moves his hands down to my jeans, undoing them before using his other hand to put mine behind my back, pushing me into the board harder to keep them from moving.

At least from here, this will make getting my knife a bit easier.

"Keep your hands behind you or you won't like the punishment." He watches me, waiting for me to acknowledge him, but I refuse to give him the satisfaction. I need him angry and off balance, so he doesn't pay attention to my small movements.

"Answer me before you regret it!" he snaps, and I pull my lips into my mouth, refusing to speak.

He growls, roughly shoving his hand into my

jeans and panties, rubbing me before thrusting two fingers inside me, making me scream out in pain from behind my lips.

Unlike when Luke touches me, I'm not wet. I don't want this.

He leans over, biting my neck as his fingers pump in and out of me, his thumb rubbing my clit and drawing pleasure from my unwilling body until I'm almost screaming from the sheer destruction of emotions coursing through me.

"That's it, Doll. You're going to cum for me, aren't you? Be a good little toy and cum all over my hand before I take this tight, perfect cunt and claim you as mine."

I whimper, trying to fight the orgasm that threatens to wash over me as my fingers finally come into contact with my knife.

Just a few more moments and I can make my move.

I watch him, waiting until he's in a vulnerable position to pounce, just like the kitty with claws that Luke refers to me as.

This asshole is about to find out what wrath actually looks like.

He growls, knowing I'm refusing to cum, and moves his one hand to his pants, quickly pulling his dick out, rubbing it as his other hand stays on me, rubbing circles around my clit, coaxing the orgasm out of me that I've been fighting.

I moan and whimper, refusing to scream from the pleasure because it's mixed with shame and disgust. It's also the perfect opportunity to attack when he groans, starting to pull his hand out of me.

Once his hand is out of my pants, I lunge for him, shoving my knife deep into his abdomen, but he doesn't scream. He looks at me with a darkness and lust as he grunts out an orgasm, his cum covering his hands as the blood trickles down to mix with it, his eyes never leaving mine.

What the fuck just happened?

I shake my head, refusing to think any more on it before pulling the knife from him, grabbing my phone from the floor and running out of the room like the devil is on my tail. His laughter floats through the air and I shiver because, if there's anyone that resembles the devil, it may very well be that man I just stabbed.

Creed
Chapter Fourteen

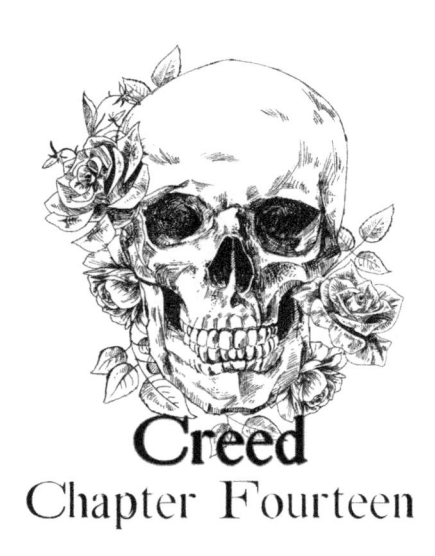

F uck.

She doesn't realize she just sealed her fate in being mine. The second she drove that knife into me, she made sure that I'd never let my pretty Doll go.

She's perfect. Perfect for me with her tight virgin pussy and her knife skills. I bet she'll cut me so good when we come together.

Just thinking about taking her, maybe having Ollie join us is enough to have my dick throbbing again.

I quickly send Ollie a text to pick me up before using my blood to jerk myself off once more, cumming into my hand in record time by digging my other hand into the stab wound to offer the pain I need.

God, she's fucking perfect.

I smirk, putting my temporarily sated dick back into my jeans before doing them up and wincing. There's fucking blood everywhere. Ollie's going to lose his shit.

"What the fuck happened to you?!" he hisses at me from the driver's seat as I plop into the passenger side, wincing a little from the pain.

Now that the buzz of adrenaline has worn off, this stings like a fucking bitch.

My Doll didn't pull any punches, and that's so fucking hot.

"I got stabbed." He sucks in a breath. "I'm fine. But can we get home so you can help me clean this? It's starting to sting like a bitch."

He narrows his eyes at me before putting the car in drive and heading back to the house. "How the fuck did you get yourself stabbed? And what were you doing here alone?! You've got to stop doing that, you stupid fucker! Look what happens when you go out on your own!" He's screeching at me and it's adorable as fuck that he's so worried about me.

"I needed to see her, Ollie. I needed to see my Doll."

"That answers why you're on campus, then," he huffs out a breath before turning his head sharply toward me. "BUT WHO THE FUCK STABBED YOU?!"

I laugh hard, groaning when pain shoots through my abdomen. "My Doll is so pretty, Ollie. You like her, right?"

"Of course I fucking like her! She's an ang— Wait. Did Lukas stab you?!"

I snort out a laugh, putting more pressure on my wound. "Nah, man. He'd never do that in public. My pretty Doll stabbed me. She's perfect," I sigh, and he slams on the brakes. "Ouch, love. Fuck! Warn a guy!" I grumble, but he doesn't say anything, just stares at me with wide eyes. "What? Why are you looking at me like that?"

"Haliee stabbed you?" His voice is monotone as he blinks, waiting for my confirmation.

"Yep. Isn't she perfect? And the orgasm. Fuck, Ollie. You have to feel her."

He blinks at me. "You had sex with Haliee, and she stabbed you?"

I pout. "No. I made her cum on my fingers, but before I got to fuck her, she stabbed me. Still came, though."

"HAVE YOU LOST YOUR FUCKING MIND, CREED?!"

Now it's my turn to blink. "Not more than usual." He growls at my attitude, giving every car that honks at him the middle finger. "Not that I'm usually the logical one, but don't you think we should…I don't know….move to the side of the road?"

"No!" he shouts, and I shrug.

"Eh, whatever."

"Creed!"

"Yeah?" He's so grumpy. Maybe I should blow him later. That usually cheers my poor Ollie up.

"Did you finger her because she asked you to?"

"Not exactly."

He groans, pulling at his hair. "So, you cornered her and did what you always do. You took what you wanted without asking." I shrug. It's not a lie. "Do you realize that's considered rape?! Fuck, Creed. You just fucked us all over for tonight."

I lift a brow. "What's tonight?"

He groans, putting the car back into drive and heading toward the house. "Tonight, is the Halloween party. Lukas is officially introducing us to Haliee."

I smile and he groans even more. "Well, then. Let the games begin."

Haliee

THE CAR RIDE is making this corset a million times more uncomfortable than it should be. Agreeing to go to this Halloween party was beyond stupid of me considering I haven't told Lukas a thing about what happened while we were apart today.

I've started having mixed emotions about it. I

did not consent to that shit, but I can't deny that it's now plaguing my fantasies.

I looked into his eyes and saw the wild in them, but I also saw something deeper. I saw obsession and longing.

I fight hard to contain the shiver that escapes me anyway.

"A little chilly, my beautiful pirate?" Lukas asks, squeezing my knee while keeping his eyes on the road.

He said we'd be meeting his brothers tonight, but it's hard to be excited when I'm filled with guilt at keeping this secret from him.

He turns off the main road onto a little dirt lane that's tucked in between the trees. Cars are already lined up on either side, and I can hear the music thumping from the house before we even get out of the car.

Lukas adjusts his "uniform" and goes to grab my hand to guide me along toward the rave taking place.

"Isn't it a little cliché to dress as a cop when you actually are one?" I ask jokingly.

"Detective, babe. I'm a detective," Lukas replies with a smirk.

We walk into the house where bodies are

packed in tighter than a jar of pickles, and head toward the kitchen to get our first round of drinks.

Always having to stay on alert, I've never really given into the temptation of alcohol, but with him by my side one can't hurt.

I run my hand over where my knife is hidden in my corset to make sure it's still secure before taking a drink and choking.

"What the fuck is this? Diesel fuel?"

He chuckles and kisses me hard. "Whiskey and coke. Here's to a good night," Lukas hollers over the music, before taking a drink of his cup without even flinching.

I toss the rest of mine back, gagging a little when the burn hits the back of my throat. Fuck's sake, brown definitely doesn't go down well.

"Is there any clear? I'm not really a fan of brown liquors, apparently," I yell to Lukas.

He does a quick check of the cups and bottle selections before he grabs a bottle of grey goose and pours me a shot.

I quickly toss it back and start relaxing as both drinks start flowing through my system.

"Let's dance. My brothers should be here soon," Lukas yells in my ear.

I nod and start dragging him toward the open

living room where grinding bodies are all over the place. Some couples are even hooking up against the walls like it's some porn set.

I pause and wait for Lukas to slide his hands around me when we start moving to the beat of *Beggin' by Måneskin*.

I feel Lukas move his hands down my hips toward my legs where the bunched-up skirt I'm wearing ends mid-thigh.

Grinding against him, I lay my head back on his shoulder and he takes the opportunity to start trailing kisses down my neck. Moving his hands under my skirt, he's leaving a trail of fire everywhere he touches.

Before he makes it any further toward where I'd like him to be, a sharp loud whistle pierces through the music, and we snap our heads toward the noise where an almost carbon copy of my man is standing. He's surrounded by guys, including the twins from class.

What has me sucking in the most ragged of breaths is the face directly behind his brother, because I've just been reunited with the devil.

The one I stabbed in the classroom before leaving him to bleed earlier.

His sinister smile is in place while his eyes devour me.

Call me a sick bitch, but I'm starting to like that look on him.

I think I may be broken.

We go to move toward them, but something or someone trips me. Before my face becomes one with the floor, Lukas grabs me and hauls me back to my feet.

Thank fuck.

"The fuck is your issue, Amber?!" Lukas yells as she looks us over with a smirk in place.

"Sorry there, Lukas. Didn't see the whore. Maybe keep her on a better leash next time. It'd be a shame for someone to have to deal with her before you had your fill and start fucking Joslyn again," Amber says smoothly.

The girl in question looks at me with so much maliciousness, I almost want to punch it off her face.

"First off, that was a onetime drunk hookup that my dick still regrets," Lukas seethes before going deadly calm. "Secondly, Haliee is so far above your level that the seven of us will never, and I really do mean never, ever come back to your group of skanks." He lets out a deep breath as anger rolls off him. "And lastly, was that a threat to my girl?"

Amber stammers and sputters as the rest of the bitches look like they want to strangle me, before she gathers enough brain cells to speak again.

"Please. I'd have to care first," she shoots back, spinning in place and heading off toward the kitchen where a bunch of football jocks are gathered.

"Stop focusing on women you view as a threat, Amber, and start focusing on the dicks that actually want to fuck you," Lukas hollers at her, and she pauses before screaming and stomping off.

Well, then. That's a side of my man I didn't know existed, and I'm seriously fucking turned on right now.

We start moving through the crowd again, heading toward the guys. I take another look at them before deciding I need a minute before facing the devil.

"I need to use the girl's room really quick," I push out in a rush, nervously bouncing on my feet.

"I'll walk you over." Lukas starts steering me toward the restroom, but I stop him.

"I got it, babe. Quick in and out to powder my nose," I soothe, taking off for the back hallway.

There's a line from hell for the one down here, so I decide to book it up the stairs and find one there instead.

I breath out a sigh of relief when I find it empty, quickly making my way in and shutting the door.

I walk over to the sink and splash some water on my face as I look at myself in the mirror above it.

Get your shit together, Haliee. Facing him is nothing compared to Dimitri.

A thump at the door makes me jump.

"Occupied!" I yell out.

"I know, Haliee." Comes a voice from the other side that chills me to the bone. Someone I don't know, but they clearly know me.

The door shoots open and one of the jocks from downstairs steps in, shutting behind him and flicking the lock.

"Time to have a little fun, miss bitch." He grins at me with a sickening look in his eyes. "You really think you're so much better than everyone else, don't you?" He prowls toward me, and I start to panic.

I know I have my knife on me, but fuck! I really don't want to stab two people in one fucking day!

Besides, this guy is fucking huge and looks deranged in a way I imagine Dimitri to be.

"What the hell are you talking about? I literally stay away from everyone and mind my own damn business." I stand up straight, fixing my skirt to make sure this asshole doesn't get a free show.

"You can't come in and just threaten Amber's very existence without consequence." He steps even closer, and I roll my eyes. He's about three feet from me now, so I still have control over my shit, but if he gets any closer, it'll be game over. "It's not like it's a hardship to fuck the new virgin to make you lose your value. You're actually pretty hot for a freak."

Before I have any time to plan or react, he lunges for me, and I can't stop the scream that comes from me as he slams into my body, and his fist connects with my jaw.

This fucking prick. He's done for once I can see straight.

I let the calm training Dad gave me take over, and act on muscle memory alone to fight back. He will not rape me.

In the back of my mind, I can't help but wonder why I didn't scream when the guy attacked me earlier, but I can focus on that later.

Right now, I need to get this prick's hands off me.

Torren

HALIEE IS A FUCKING stunner even from this distance, and I know we're all completely fucked.

I can tell just from the way Luke looks at her that he's already gone completely gaga.

Before we can reach them, Haliee falls, making Creed lurch forward before wincing and grabbing his stomach. I wonder what the hell he did to himself as Ollie pulls him back and whispers something in his ear to make him seethe, but he stays put.

Thank fucking Christ.

The last thing we need is for him to piss Lukas off or kill the mayor's daughter.

Yeah, Amber is the mayor's fucking daughter.

We've been trying to come up with a plan to get rid of her since Cord cut her off after Creed told us about her plan to drug Haliee and have someone rape her. That alone puts her on our kill list, but we have to bide our time with her.

Not even Luke could get us out of that political shitstorm.

My brother looks ready to kill as Haliee leaves him to go do whatever it is chicks do, and we reach him.

"Hey, bro." I gather him in a quick hug before pounding our knuckles together.

"Hey. Glad you guys made it."

The six of us grunt.

"What the fuck just happened with my Doll?" Creed is seething, and Luke narrows his eyes at him.

"She's not *your* anything." Luke goes to take a step toward him when we hear a scream.

"Was that?"

"Haliee!" Lukas and I break into a run at the same time, heading toward the stairs. The sound was muffled and quiet, so there's no way it was coming from down here.

"If she's hurt, I'm gutting you like a fish," Creed threatens Luke, and I almost trip over my feet for a second.

What the fuck?

Lukas doesn't answer, just leads the way up the

stairs where sounds of a fight are coming from behind a closed door.

"Haliee!" Lukas barks, banging on the door when it doesn't open for him.

She doesn't answer as we hear more grunts and muffled cries from behind the door. The noises have my heart racing, and every nerve on edge.

A quick look at the rest of the guys shows that they're having the same struggle as we listen to her fighting and cursing along with a guy slinging threats at her.

"Move away from the door, Doll!" Creed bellows, stomping toward us and shoving me out of the way.

They share a look before counting to three and ramming the door together with their shoulders. Ollie hisses out a breath at the pain they're probably feeling from that hit, but the door barely budges.

Lining up and hitting it again, there's a loud crack that echoes through the upstairs, but I know no one downstairs is going to care. They're too drunk to figure out what's happening.

"One more," Luke barks.

Creed growls, nodding in agreement before they count to three again, running into the door and almost falling into the bathroom, panting from the exertion of breaking it down.

We all freeze at the scene before us.

Haliee is standing over some fuck's body with a knife to his throat, and I'm instantly fucking hard.

God, my brother is going to kill me for getting a stiffy over his girl, but how can I not? She's dressed in a sexy corset type pirate costume. To add flame to the fire that's my libido, her skirt is torn, her hair a mess, and she has specks of blood covering her chest and face.

I know I'm not the only guy here sporting a boner over this sinful goddess.

That boner dies a little when I take in the puffiness of her jaw a split second before Creed does.

"You're a dead man," Creed swears, lunging for the fucker so fast Haliee barely has a chance to step back before he's on him. He punches him repeatedly, past the point of unconsciousness.

"Creed. Step off!" Mathias barks as Luke goes over to Haliee, holding his hands up like he's afraid she's going to flee like a skittish rabbit or attack him next. Creed glares at Mathias, looking toward Haliee and Luke.

"He fucking hit her, Matt."

Mathias nods. "I'm aware, and he will die for

that." He glances at Haliee and winces, her eyes wide. "But not now and not here."

Creed looks to Haliee once more before deflating and climbing off the asshole. "Fine." He's not happy about it, but he's never happy when any of us stop him from playing with his toys.

"Hey, Scratch. Are you okay?" Lukas is right in front of her now, still holding his hands up as he waits for her.

"I'm... I'm fine, I think." She shakes her head before folding the knife back up and slipping it into her boobs, making us all groan a little. "Sorry, he just— he came in here and threatened a bunch of stuff and I...I reacted." She's still staring at the fucker on the ground with wide eyes. "Are you... are you really going to kill him?" She doesn't look at anyone except Creed when she asks that.

I can tell I'm not the only one confused by this, but Creed plays along with a devious smirk.

"Of course I am, Doll. He hurt you. He can't live after touching you."

She snorts, swallowing before her eyes move to my brother. "Hey," she whispers. He looks between her and Creed before pulling her into a tight hug.

"Hey, baby. I've got you," he soothes her, and Ollie snorts.

"Not to be the bearer of bad news or whatever, but it didn't look like she needed our help."

We all turn to stare at him, blinking.

"What are you talking about? He tried to rape her!" Barren barks, and Ollie snorts.

"And he would have gotten stabbed. Hell, he wouldn't have even been the first person she's stabbed today." The second he says it, his eyes grow wide. "Shit," he squeaks, and Creed starts laughing hysterically, gripping his stomach to try and ease whatever pain he's in.

"He has a point," Creed points out, but we're all staring at the two of them like they've lost their minds.

"Are you both drunk?" Corden questions, and Haliee starts sobbing.

"Luke, don't hate me. I wanted to tell you and I was going to...I just wanted us to have this night first." She's wailing in his arms, and the poor bastard looks so fucking confused.

"Haliee," I say her name, and her wet eyes meet mine while she shakes in Luke's arms. "Hi, I'm Torren. This oaf's brother."

She sniffs and offers me a small smile. "Hi."

God, her voice is like a fucking angel, isn't it? Smooth and raspy like some sort of sexy vixen.

"Hey. So, Luke and the rest of us," I pause looking to Creed and Ollie. "Well, maybe most of us...we're all just a bit lost. Think you could fill us in on what's going on so we can help you feel better?"

She blinks, sniffling and looking up to Luke who is watching her with concern. She opens her mouth to answer when Ollie pipes up.

"Oh! She just stabbed Creed when he tried to force sex on her." He shrugs, but everyone goes so silent you could hear a pin drop.

Ah fuck.

Lukas
Chapter Fifteen

I had to have heard Ollie wrong.

"Say what now?" I try to keep my anger in check, but I'm so close to murdering Creed right along with the fuckwad on the ground, it's not even funny.

"I'm sorry, Lukas! I swear I was going to tell you. I just didn't want our date ruined!" Haliee is freaking the fuck out in my arms, and as badly as I want to be angry with her for not telling me, I also kind of get it.

I'm still upset, though.

"Baby, look at me." I fight to keep the anger from my voice. When her poor red and wet eyes meet mine, my entire heart fucking crumbles.

"Luke," she says my name barely above a whisper, pain and fear so evident I can't stop the anger from seeping through.

"Did you ask him to touch you?" I practically spit the question, then wince.

Her eyes go wide, and she tries to pull away from me, but I don't let her. "Never." She's so hurt right now that she won't stop fighting me. "Let me go, Lukas. If you honestly think I'd ever purposely betray you then you don't even know me. Let me fucking go!" she screams at me, trying to pull away, but I refuse to lose her over this shit.

"I'm not letting you run from this, Haliee."

"She said let her go, asshole. Let go of my Doll before I add you to the list of pricks in this room that are about to be dead," Creed barks at me, and she goes stiff in my arms.

I really don't fucking like it.

"You!" she growls like some sort of feral cat. "This is all your fucking fault!" she screeches at him, trying to fight to get through me, and I go from holding her to stop her from running, to holding her back from attacking Creed.

"Someone want to tell me what the fuck happened?!" I bark, holding my girl back.

"This motherfucker cornered me in the classroom when I went to get my phone and forced his hand down my pants!" Haliee is fighting against my hold, and I seriously want to let her go right now. "Then he forced an orgasm out of me while violating me when I said no."

I snap.

"Creed!" we all holler at him.

Well, everyone except Oliver who seems to just be watching the show for his own entertainment.

"Have you lost your mind?!" Corden shouts.

"What is wrong with you?!" Barren sneers.

"That's not okay." Torren says, trying to be the calm one.

"That goes against everything we stand for, Creed!" Mathias barks the loudest, and Creed winces.

"She's my Doll. I needed her." He looks pleadingly at me and Haliee, but she's not backing down.

"Get fucked, asshole! If I wanted you to touch me, I'd have asked!" she spits out.

"If you want anyone to touch you, you come to me, Scratch," I growl before I think better of it.

Looking at my brothers, I can tell they all want her. I'm probably going to have to share her eventually if it's what she wants. But right now? Not a fucking chance.

"How did that turn into you stabbing him?" my brother asks her in a soft tone, instantly calming her again.

I hate to admit it, but fuck. He's definitely got one hell of a soft spot and gentleness for her that I've never seen in him before.

She smiles at him, but it's not the sweet girl I'm used to.

"While he had my arms pinned behind me, I pissed him off by refusing to cum. It was enough of a distraction he didn't notice my micro movements as he got angrier." She smirks at Creed who's watching her with lust and obsession so clear it makes my stomach turn.

"And?" Torren questions, asking her to continue.

She groans, stopping the fight in my arms and turning around to face me. Her eyes are full of brokenness and fear, and I sigh.

"It's okay, baby. I might be a little pissed you didn't tell me, but I promise I'm not going anywhere."

She sniffles before throwing herself into my

arms. I lift her up as her legs wrap around my waist and she kisses my neck, crying.

"I love you, Lukas," she purrs through tears, and I swear we all freeze. No one outside of us seven, and my own father, has ever used that word with us. Told us that we're loved.

It's a completely foreign concept, but I know in my chest that I love her too, so I don't hold back.

"I love you too, Haliee Morgan," I confess, holding her tight against me. "Baby, I need you to finish this story so I can get you out of here," I whisper, and she nods into my neck before pulling her head back to look at me.

"As I said, I pissed him off enough that he wouldn't notice me moving ever so slightly. Anyway, when he finally let up to get his dick out," she pauses, scrunching up her nose in disgust. But there's something else there too. Desire and worry. At least some small part of her wanted, and still wants, Creed in all his fucked-up ways, but that's a conversation for her and I alone.

Later.

"And?" Torren prompts, and she turns her head to look at him.

"And that's when I stabbed him, and he came

like a fucking weirdo. Apparently, pain is his thing." She shrugs and it's so nonchalant that we all burst out laughing before I sober up.

"Creed," I growl his name, my tone dangerous, and they all know it. "You ever touch my girl without her permission again, and I will help her hide your body."

His eyes go wide before a spark of mischief appears. "You got it, Lukey pookey." He winks, and Haliee starts giggling like a fucking schoolgirl at the worst nickname in fucking history.

Fucking great.

Corden

. . .

By the time Luke and Haliee leave the party, it's time for us to do our thing with the waste of life on the floor. He tried to rape her and for that, he dies.

I have no doubt that Amber had something to do with this, and it makes me physically fucking ill knowing I ever touched that cunt.

Truth be told, now that I've seen how fucking hot Haliee looks with blood on her, and know she can wield a knife enough to actually stab Creed, not to mention bring this asshole to the ground and hold it against his throat?

I don't think I'll ever want another woman again. Not the way I want her. And ain't that just some fucked up shit?

She's one hundred and ten percent off fucking limits, and now my dick and heart are filled with need for the one chick I can't fucking have.

Fucking perfect.

"Alright, everyone glove up and let's get this shit done." We all nod at Mathias, pulling the spare gloves we always keep handy.

You never fucking know when you're going to need them.

"I'll stay here and clean up any traces of him," I say, and Mathias nods.

"Good. Ollie and Creed can go set up the warehouse."

Creed cackles with glee. "On it! So fucking on it."

Once him and Oliver leave, he turns to Barren. "Help me get him outside through the window." He grimaces remembering we're on the second floor. "Actually, you go downstairs and outside, then let me know you're at the bottom of this window. Cord and I will lower him down to you, then I'll come down and we can put him in the car."

Barren nods.

"Someone needs to get his keys, phone, and drive his car somewhere to burn them. Just make sure his last known location isn't here," I point out and Mathias nods.

"I know. I'll do it while Barren takes him to the warehouse. When we're done there, we can burn him and the car at the same time so there's zero evidence of us being involved, but he's still found."

"I fucking hate that he has to be found at all. It's easier when they disappear," my twin growls, and I nod in agreement.

"Yeah, but he's one of Amber's pussy-whipped shit heads. She knows he was here, so we have to let him be found," I say and Matt agrees.

"She'll know it's us, but if his body is found they'll have zero way to trace it to us. If the fucker disappeared completely, she could throw up a shitstorm against us." He scrubs his hand down his face. "This way is the safest option. She can't bring law enforcement down on our heads with a body and absolutely no proof, but she could if he just vanished." He shakes his head. "We'll frame that fucker we killed a few days ago. They'll never find his body, and just assume he's on the run. We have all the DNA evidence we could possibly need for that."

We both nod in agreement, little smirks on our faces before we get to work getting the asshole out of here.

Once we've lowered him to the ground outside, I change my gloves and grab the small spray bottle we also carry with us. It's a mixture of paint thinner and gasoline to make blood tests inconclusive. I set out spraying the small splatters and wiping them clean with bleach.

It's not like there's a shit ton of blood to get rid of. All she did was break his nose, but it's always better to be safe rather than sorry.

Once I'm satisfied everything is degraded and cleaned, I put everything I used into a zippy bag, then stroll back to the party like nothing ever happened before heading to the car where Barren is waiting.

Like I said. We're prepared for every single fucking outcome. Even our trunks have hidden compartments with a roll of plastic, so blood doesn't get on our shit.

We've totally got this shit.

Haliee
Chapter Sixteen

Silence sucks. So much for my first official date going off without a hitch.

Actually, you know what pisses me off the most? I fucking loved this corset, and now that prick's blood is all over it.

Should have moved to the side before breaking his nose.

Lukas drives us straight to a quiet lookout I've never seen, but that doesn't surprise me since I'm relatively new here.

What does surprise me is the fact that he's refusing to even speak to me.

Like, fuck. If you don't want to talk, can we just go home?

"Lukas," I whisper, staring out the window. I can see him grinding his teeth together from the corner of my eye, his jaw tense.

"Haliee, I'm trying really hard to not lose my shit on you right now." I whimper before I can think better on it, and his head snaps toward me. "Why didn't you tell me that you were attacked today?" His voice is hard and demanding, but his eyes are soft.

"Because, Luke. You never would have taken me out tonight."

He grunts, snorting before shaking his head. "Not a great excuse, babe."

It's my turn to narrow my eyes.

"Maybe not for you and your old ass, but did you even think about the fact that this is my first date? Ever?!"

His whole body deflates. "Fuck," he groans. "I'm sorry, Scratch. I know this meant a lot to you."

I nod, crossing my arms over my boobs. "Good."

"But if you had told me who and what they did, I would have known it was Creed's psychotic ass and just beat the shit out of him."

I blink at him. "You realize I didn't know who he was at the time, right?" I ask, my voice filled with annoyance. "I had no idea how to process everything that happened in such a short amount of time."

"What's there to process?" he questions, and I sigh.

"He was psychotic and forced himself on me, but a part of me wasn't afraid. I can't explain it, okay? I already fucking hate myself for letting him make me cum." He growls, and I hold up my hand. "Bad choice of words. I fought it so fucking hard, but it was only a matter of time before he got it out of me when I was incapable of fighting back." I sigh. "I had to bide my time. And if the fact that I stabbed him isn't enough proof for you that I didn't want it, I don't know what is."

He watches me for a moment, darkness like I've never seen crossing his eyes. Lukas is usually an easy going, fun guy, but whatever is going on in his mind right now is a side of him I haven't come to know yet.

No time like the present, I guess.

"Haliee, I'm going to ask you something and I need you to be one hundred percent honest with me." His eyes are staring into mine and I swallow, nodding.

"Anything."

"Do you want Creed?"

I wrinkle my nose. "No. At least, not the way I want you." I move over to straddle his lap, my ass hitting the horn as I try to get comfy, and he grunts. "You make me feel safe and secure. Like I'm beautiful and you'd do anything for me. That I'm actually desired." I kiss him, and his hands land on my hips.

"That's because you are, babe. All of that is true to how I feel for you." He shakes his head, his hands squeezing my hips. "There's a lot you don't know about me, Scratch."

I shrug. "Nothing you tell me could ever change how I look at you. You put me first, and that's all that matters."

He gives me a soft smile, mischief twinkling in his eyes. "Before you came along, my brothers were all I knew. I lived and breathed to take care of them."

"I like that I mean something to you," I tell him with a smile, rolling my hips against his dick.

"You mean more than I could ever explain. I've never done this before."

I lift my eyebrow. "Sex?"

He laughs hard, his dick growing in his pants. "Uh, no, babe. Sorry to say it, but I've had lots of sex." I scowl and he laughs harder, his hand coming up to my cheek. "But that's all it ever was. Sex. There was nothing meaningful there." He leans in to kiss me softly. "You're different. The second I laid eyes on you, I knew I was fucked, Haliee. You're so fucking gorgeous."

I giggle and lean in. "Yeah?"

"Yeah, babe." His hands move down my back and cup my ass, gently rocking me against his huge dick. "Then I was forced to get to know you, and I was done for. I've never met any—wait—did you say we're having sex tonight?"

I smile down at him, shaking my head at how long it took him to figure that out. "Well, yeah. I kinda hoped we would, anyway."

He groans, lifting his hips to rub against my core. "Fuck. Are you sure you're ready for that after what Creed did to you today?" His eyes flash with anger and annoyance, but I cup his face in my hands.

"It's because of what he did that I know I want this. Whatever happens, I know without a doubt that I want and need you to be my first." I swallow heavily, afraid of how he will react to my next words. "Was I afraid of your friend? Yes, but not like I was of that asshole tonight." I bite my lip trying to figure out how to explain it.

"But you're attracted to him," Lukas points out, and I look into his eyes for a moment before nodding.

"Yes." He's silent for a few seconds, but I can feel how much he still wants me. "I also got the feeling that he doesn't actually want to harm me. Not in a bad way, at least."

He lifts an eyebrow. "You stabbed him, Scratch."

I groan, laying my forehead against his. "I'm aware of that. He scared me and I reacted, but…it's hard to explain, I guess? I think maybe the fierceness or obsession in his voice drew me in." I frown, and see his lips twitch.

"He's most definitely obsessed with you. I think they all are at this point."

"Yeah, okay." I roll my eyes, and his hands tighten around my ass.

"Do not belittle your self-worth, Haliee. You're hot, and sweet, and so caring. You're the opposite of anything we've ever known, and I can't blame them for being into you, too." His hands tighten some more until I'm squirming. "Doesn't mean I won't kill the fuckers for touching you without your permission."

I deflate. "You don't want to be with me anymore, do you?" I move my eyes to look down between us.

"Oh, Scratch, you're always going to be mine. And to prove it, I'm going to take this sweet cherry of yours, so you never forget who you belong to," he growls before quickly pulling my mouth to his.

Sweet fucking hell. That's hot.

His tongue pushes into my mouth hard and fast, tangling with mine and I groan. Fuck, he tastes incredible, like I never want to go without this every day for the rest of my fucking life.

His one hand cups the back of my neck possessively as he reaches between us, stroking me through my panties, and I moan into him.

"Luke!" I whine and he chuckles, thrusting his hips up against my ass.

"That's it, baby. I want you to cum all over my hand, screaming my name before I finally claim you." He ends his speech by pushing my panties to the side as his fingers start dragging through the slickness that's only there for him.

Fuck, I'm so wet I'm pretty sure sex wouldn't even hurt that much right now, and I want it hard.

I want him to claim me so hard and deep that our souls are seared together for all eternity. I want him to be forever mine as much as I am his.

"Lukas, baby," I moan as he slides one finger into my core before pulling it back out and adding a second.

"So fucking wet and tight." He grinds his erection against my ass, groaning when I dig my nails into his shoulders.

"Please. Oh, god, yes! Oh, shit," I curse and he chuckles, picking up the speed of his thrusting fingers.

"That's it, Scratch. Cum for me so I know you're relaxed and ready to take me."

"I'm ready now!" I whine, and he kisses me hard before pressing his thumb lightly against my clit.

"I said cum for me, baby. If you want my cock inside you, you need to fucking cum for me," he growls, his movements growing faster until I'm spiralling over the edge.

"Yes, right there. Yes, yes!!!!!" I scream as my orgasm takes over, closing my eyes against the blinding pleasure as he drags it out, his fingers slowing but never leaving me until I'm lax in his arms.

"Fuck, that was beautiful." He kisses my nose and I chuckle, wiggling my ass on his dick, making him groan. "Backseat and panties off. Right the fuck now." He slaps my ass and I hiss, my pussy flooding even more from his commanding tone.

"Yes, Sir!" I mock, saluting him before biting my lip and lifting off him to make my way to the backseat. "Dammit. Shouldn't you have a bigger car?" I groan, struggling to get to the back seat while he opens the door.

"No." He slams the door shut as my ass hits the seat. I pout for a moment before the back door opens and he's struggling with the button on his pants.

"Oh!" I groan, and he smirks at me before his eyes travel lower.

"Panties off, Scratch."

Right! I scramble, pulling my panties down my hips before lifting my knees to get them off over my ankles and lean back on the seat. Spreading my knees wide, I move my hand to my pussy and gasp at how slick I feel.

"Like this?" My voice is husky, and he growls, roughly pulling his cock out of his pants.

"Just like that, baby. Are you ready for me? Last chance to back out."

I moan, circling my fingers over my clit. "So ready."

He curses, moving into the back seat until he pulls me to the edge, my ass almost hanging out the door.

"Good. I'm not going to be gentle, baby. I fucking need you so badly."

I nod and he pulls my hand away before sliding his dick through my wetness. "Lukas!" I moan, and he leans down to kiss me, his tip resting at my entrance.

"Fuck, baby. I love you," he whispers to me, breaching my entrance just slightly.

"I love you too," I gasp and he bites my lip before thrusting into me in one swift movement. The pain searing through me.

"Omg!" I scream as tears burn the back of my eyes. "Fuck. Shit!" I curse, and he chuckles into my neck before groaning.

"Fucking hell. You feel so god damned good, baby," he groans. I try moving my hips to get more comfortable, but he bites my neck. "Stay fucking still," he growls, and I roll my eyes.

"Then fucking move, Lukas. I'm not going to break."

He pulls his head up and looks down into my

eyes. "Yeah?" he taunts, and I smirk, wrapping my legs around his hips, ignoring the pressure that's still there.

"Yeah. Now move and claim me like you promised."

He doesn't need to be told twice.

Pulling out of me, he thrusts back in and this time I moan, digging my fingers through his hair. The pressure and pain mix with pleasure as he moves inside me.

"Oh yeah, that's it, baby. No one around to hear us. Let me hear you scream." His voice is hoarse as he continues to move his hips against me, sliding in and out at a fast, brutal pace.

"Lukas! Right there," I groan, lifting my hips to meet his as he hits a spot deep inside me. Pressure starts building in my lower belly like I've never felt. "Please, oh God," I moan, and he wraps his arm around my lower back, lifting me higher.

"That's it, baby. Let go for me," he groans as I start writhing beneath him.

"I...I need." I gasp as his teeth sink into my neck. "Fucking YES!!!" I scream as everything goes black.

Pleasure explodes through me like never before

as his movements become erratic, pushing into me once more before pulling out.

His cum splashes hot against my core as he groans. "Holy fuck, Haliee."

I come back to the present, watching his hand move up and down his shaft as small ropes of cum continue to shoot out of him, and smile.

"That's messy," I whisper.

He blinks at me a few times before barking out a laugh, collapsing against the open car door.

"Fuck. I didn't even think about a condom. I'm sorry, Scratch."

I smile, shifting around and wincing at the soreness between my thighs. "It's fine, Luke. I don't regret a second of that."

He quickly adjusts himself back into his pants, doing them up before he leans down to cup my cheek. "I'll never regret making you mine. You're fucking incredible, you know that?"

I feel the blush then gag at the feeling of the cum on me. "Babe, I love you. That was amazing and something I definitely want to do again, but you need to help me clean this up because…gross."

He chuckles, shaking his head and giving me a quick kiss before pulling his shirt off. "You got it, baby."

Haliee
Chapter Seventeen

Please pick up the phone.

God, I feel like such a fucking girl right now, but Kristen is my first real friend and I need to tell someone about losing my v-card to Lukas last night.

"Hey, girl, what's up?" she answers the phone a little breathless, and I squeal.

"Thank fuck you answered!" I screech, and she chuckles.

"Uh, yeah. Of course, I answered. Are you okay?" she questions me, and I sigh.

"Totally fine, just need to have a girl chat." I can practically feel her smiling through the phone.

We've only been friends for a couple of months, and with the whirlwind that is my life, we don't get to hang out nearly as much as I'd like, but she's always smiling.

I kind of envy that about her.

"Okay, you've got me. Hit me with it."

I take a deep breath, feeling my own smile. "I had sex with Lukas last night," I whisper scream into the phone, and it's her turn to squeal, making me laugh.

"Holy shit! What was it like?"

I blink. "You've never had sex?" I ask.

I shouldn't find that so hard to believe. Not everyone is only a virgin at eighteen because they've been on the run from some crazy Russian creep.

She snorts down the line. "Babe, I've had plenty of sex, but not with someone as old and hot as Lukas Michaels."

I laugh. "I can't believe you just said that to me."

"Hey, I can't deny the guy is hotter than a cover model. So, tell me!"

"It was kind of hot as fuck, actually." I giggle.

"That much is obvious! How could it not be with the way he looks at you? Babe, that's a five alarm fire no one could put out."

I shake my head, laughing at her remarks. "The Halloween party was kind of a bust," I start to explain. There's no way I'm getting into the specifics of that asshole.

Luke had already said they were taking care of him, and I'm all for it.

Whatever they do to the wannabe rapist fuck is fine with me.

"That sucks."

I shrug, doesn't matter that she can't see me. "Anyway, we went driving and he eventually parked and I kind of...jumped him?" I wince, and she's completely silent for a second before bursting into raucous fits of laughter.

"Damn, that's amazing. So, you literally lost it to a super hot, older guy in his car. I think you're my fucking hero."

I laugh with her, telling her about everything that happened, trying to not get overly detailed, but come on! I have a hot as fuck boyfriend with a big dick. I'm going to brag.

We talk for probably half an hour before she has to let me go. When we hang up, I can't seem to lose the smile that's permanently on my face.

"Come here, Hope." I lay down on the bed and she jumps up with me, curling into my side and purring away while we wait for Lukas to come back up with the lunch he insisted on making me.

I really do love him.

Barren

MY PHONE BLARES to life before my alarm, waking me out of the nightmare I relive every night. I sit up in bed with the sheets tangled in a lump at my feet, feeling the sweat pour off my chest.

Every night it's the same thing. My past comes back to haunt me like they can still torture me from beyond the grave.

Why me? Why couldn't I have been born into a happy, loving, and caring family instead of having narcissistic parents who preferred to use their emotions as weapons against us.

Instead of being locked in a dark and damp basement, begging and crying. Wondering if I would even get to eat that day.

I promise I'll be better, mommy, please!?!

I punch myself in the side of the head, trying to shut the memories off.

I'm not that weak and pathetic child anymore, and they can't hurt us ever again. So why can't I live it down.

PTSD is what the doctors say. We've all been diagnosed with it from our childhood traumas, but we use it to fuel our fight against other crooked and fucked up bastards who have no business existing in the world.

My phone blares again, helping me shake off the remainder of the haunting memories as I pick it up.

My heart begins to race for a completely new reason this time.

Mathias:

Code Angel. Meet at track. Stay hidden and use the paths.

. . .

Jumping out of bed, I quickly get dressed before slamming on my running shoes and heading out the door in under five minutes.

The track has been abandoned for years, and it's the perfect place to meet up without anyone else seeing us.

It's technically condemned, and most people stay far away from the dangerous terrain within the fences. Not us, though.

When we realized that Haliee was an innocent and was going to be with Lukas for the long haul, we created CODE ANGEL as a way of letting everyone in the group know that she was in danger.

This is the first time we've had to use it, and I worry what could be wrong.

I pump my arms faster, tearing down the path as fear tries to grip me.

It's still dark enough out that I can barely see a thing in front of me, but I could run these paths in my sleep without fail.

Breaking through the trees and foliage, I make it in record time. The second I'm through the fence, I see Mathias leaning against the old announcer's booth to my right and make my way over.

"Not your worst time, but I think you could

have done better," he pops off at me, and I narrow my eyes at him.

"I think I liked it better when you didn't speak much," I shoot back.

He just smirks and waves his hand for me to follow him.

"I've been keeping a close eye on you guys since the Halloween party last week, and there's been a strange guy following Haliee and Luke, as well as you and Corden when you're on campus."

I suck in a sharp breath because this is a first.

Normally when people hear of the Deadly Seven and the things we're capable of, they're running in the opposite direction.

"You think he's extra detail on her case?" I ask and he shrugs, looking out into the darkness.

"I can't be one hundred percent, but I do know he's been meeting with agent shady ass too." Mathias clucks his tongue.

"Lukas said Haliee and her Dad don't trust the guy either," I point out, and he nods in agreement.

"I don't think they're far off the mark. The guy seems shady as fuck, but he's never in town long that I'm aware of, and Ollie hasn't found anything on him yet."

"What's the plan then?" I question, curious on why extra detail would be brought in. Daniels is here as well as having Lukas on her almost every second of the day. Even the house has local officers watching when anyone is home.

Another agent wouldn't make sense. Not unless something else is going down that no one is aware of.

"We need to get everyone together for a family meeting without anyone wanting to kill each other. I'm not convinced that's possible with Creed and Luke right now." He sighs, shaking his head. "But for now, we need to go on as though nothing has changed. Can't give the fucker a heads up that we're onto him. I want to watch it play out for a while."

"I can work on that meeting. Though I'm a little curious why you wanted to meet out here?" He could have told me this at home just as easily.

"Well, if you're thinking what I am, then maybe these agents know something, or someone is coming to harm Haliee. I need you to take Ollie's new little cameras on your run this morning. Start setting them up in different locations so we can have more eyes everywhere." He hands me a bag of Ollie's little cameras that are smaller than the size of Lego blocks.

"Here, Ollie should be calling any minute so he can guide you to the best location points." He finishes by reaching in his jeans pocket and pulling out an earpiece.

Once it's connected to my phone, I give Mathias a quick goodbye before my phone lights up with Ollie's name and I answer it.

"Good morning, Barney Boy, how'd you sleep? Any good nightmares?" he immediately quips.

"How the fuck can you have this much energy at five in the morning, Ollie? It's not human. For fuck's sake just try and at least act tired for my sake," I grumble.

"Don't worry, sunshine. I have plenty of energy for us all. Now, I need these cameras on the different trails around the house, and then some on the roads. There's already plenty in town, so don't worry about heading in that direction."

I hear him tapping away on his keyboard, likely mapping out the locations.

"Got it. Can you do me a solid while I'm doing this, though? We need a family meeting today," I ask, because if anyone can make this happen it's

Oliver fucking Weever. "Preferably without Creed in a hostile mood?" I further iterate.

"Already on top of it. Try to be back here by noon," Ollie says, still tapping away without a care in the world.

Oliver
Chapter Eighteen

Flicking my eyes between the computer screens, I check to make sure each and every camera Barren sets up is working properly and in the right position.

I love these little fuckers that I've designed, but I'm still trying to stretch my brain to get audio included in them. I just haven't quite figured it out yet, so for now they're video feed only.

Still helpful, but annoying for me.

I'm currently sitting in the basement because I claimed it as my own personal 'bat cave' if you will. No one comes down here but me. Not even Creed.

My phone goes off, reminding me it's time for the family meeting. We even have a surprise little guest with us this time. It's probably the first meeting of many that she will be in attendance for.

The guys need Creed to cooperate today, and there's only one way to make that happen.

Having Haliee here means he won't be…well, more Creed than normal.

So, her being here is for the best, even if the guys don't see that at the start. Plus, I really just want to see her again.

Just thinking about her in that pirate costume, crouched over home dude's body with her knife to his jugular makes my cock immediately harden, and that's a first for me.

I've never been with a woman or really desired to be, either. It's always been Creed and sometimes Cord when he wants to join, or he needs the release from someone he can trust.

I don't consider myself gay because I find women attractive, but I've never had this level of need and desire for one before I saw her like that on Halloween.

She was like some avenging goddess, blessed in her enemy's blood with the promise of pain shining in her baby blues.

One look. That's all it took, and I was a fucking goner.

I hop up out of my chair and head up from the basement to make sure everyone is in attendance. Barren is almost done anyway, so he'll be here in less than ten minutes.

I note everyone spread around the living room with the exception of Lukas, Haliee, and Barren, and make my way over toward the couch.

Each one of them is glaring daggers at Creed while he does nothing but smirk at them in his psychotic way.

Fuck, he looks delicious.

"Ollie. Please tell me you didn't call us all here to discuss your burning-when-you-piss problem you so lovingly sent to the group chat, and then proceeded to lock us all out of our accounts," Torren says breaking the silence.

I ignore the snide comment as he baits me.

"Actually, I need to have a word with everyone. It's about Haliee," Mathias says, making all heads snap in his direction.

"What's going on with my Doll?" Creed snarls.

"Shoot me in the fucking face. Not this again!?!" Corden says, throwing his hands up.

"Watch your tongue before I cut it out of you, whore," Creed growls back at Corden.

"Call me a whore all you want, at least I don't

need to bleed my partners out to get off," Corden huffs out.

"ENOUGH!" Torren booms, standing up from the couch he's sitting on. "If there's something up with Haliee, we need to fucking focus and going at it like five-year-old children isn't helping. Mathias, explain," he bites out, rightly shutting everyone down.

"Yeah, what's going on with me?" Haliee's voice drifts from the doorway.

This time all heads snap in her direction, jaws dropping to the floor.

Haliee blushes a little at the attention, but she straightens her spine and looks us all in the eyes.

"Don't stop on my account," she says, looking all kinds of pissed off with her fists clenched at her sides.

Lukas is standing behind her looking equally violent.

"I knew this was a bad fucking idea," he grumbles out before nudging her in the door.

He directs her toward me, and she sits down glaring at Mathias.

He clears his throat, looking uncomfortable for the first time in his life.

Creed looks like he's getting ready to go all

caveman and drag her away back to his room. And Torren is all but openly admiring her.

Cord, well he's always horny around women so his lusty look is no surprise to me.

Animals. All of them.

"Welcome to our home, Haliee. Can I get you something to drink? Eat? A new boyfriend? I'm available, you know. Totes better than that sack of shit named Lukas. I won't tell him I'm better," I crack out.

Haliee throws her head back laughing, and I have to shift to hide my quickly thickening length at how gorgeous she is.

"I'm good, thank you. It's Oliver, right? I'm still sifting through names," she says, blushing again.

"You can call me anything you want," I quip back with a wink. "But most everyone calls me Ollie."

She laughs again, and I can't help the smile that leaves me when Lukas starts growling like the asshole he is.

Motherfucker is going to learn to share.

"You don't want me, Ollie. I'm trash. Damaged goods," she states like she's trying to curb my flirting.

"Well, as an advocate for the environment it's my duty to pick you up then," I shoot back.

"You smooth fucker!" she starts laughing again.

"Can we get back to the topic at hand?" Lukas grits out.

"Ah, yeah, yes. Um, I needed to meet with you…" Mathias starts but is interrupted by the front door banging open.

Lukas shoves Haliee behind him, pushing her into my side. I throw my arms around her turning my back toward the action to act as the shield he knew I would be for her.

Torren, Lukas, Corden, and Creed all jump up, pointing guns and knives toward the door, ready to take on whatever dumbass decided to come play in the devil's den today.

Barren throws his hands up wide-eyed and impressed as I look back on them.

"Well, hello to you too, fuckers. Where's the fire?" Barren drawls out.

Haliee has her own knife drawn that she produced from out of nowhere. I really want to know where she hides that thing.

"Well, shit, babe. Trying to protect me?" I ask her.

She's trembling slightly which makes me uneasy, so I gently move away and give her a little distance.

"Hey, it's good. Everyone here just wants to protect you," I whisper gently.

She looks lost as she stares around the room at the brutes that are lowering their weapons and trading shit with one another. I cuddle her back in my arms, sitting down and placing her on my lap to rub small circles on her back.

Lukas looks back at us and winces a little, realizing his mistake.

Then he looks down right pissed over his girl in my arms, so I do what I do best.

Smirk.

I hate to admit that Haliee's now really protecting me by acting as a shield because, if this fucker could shoot me right now, he would.

"Hey, babe….I kinda need you to save me," I mock whisper, and she laughs so hard she snorts and it's literally the most adorable shit I've ever heard.

"Something tells me you're a big bad boy all on your own, Oliver Weever." I blink at her use of my real name. No one calls me by my full name. Not since my parents, but as I wait for the fingers of dread and panic to grip my spine, they never come.

Smiling down at her, I tell her the truth.

"You're a fucking angel."

"Can I have my girl back now, Ollie?" It's really not a question, and she rolls her eyes at Lukas as he pulls her back into his arms.

"Aww, baby, don't be jealous. You know you get all the best parts of me." She winks at him before standing on her tip toes to kiss him, and I know we're all thinking the same thing.

"You fuckwad! She's my Doll!" Creed bellows, jumping up like he's going to hit him, but Haliee turns around calm as ever, holding her hand up and halting his advance.

"Firstly, I'm not a toy, so fuck you." That gets some chuckles out of everyone. "Secondly, I'm his girl and I *chose* to give him my all." She shrugs, staring Creed down, and I see him panting with the need to devour her. Tonight should be fun. "And lastly, if, and that's a BIG if, I decide I want more than just Luke, you're going to have to work your ass off for it because you're a sick fuck." She beams at him as we all blink, and Lukas bends down to kiss her neck.

"Well said, baby. I love you," Lukas whispers.

She moans, and I see everyone adjusting themselves as slyly as they can. We're all a bunch of horny fuckers for this girl.

"Right. Can we all get back on track now?" Mathias clears his throat, and I have to hide the grin that's creeping along my face.

Haliee

"Let's," I agree with Mathias, and we all get seated.

Lukas is holding me on his lap like I'm his most prized possession and he never wants to be apart from me.

I'm not upset about it either.

"Okay. Barren just finished putting Ollie's hidden cameras in a bunch of other spots, so we now have eyes on the entire town to track this shady fuck."

I narrow my eyes as Luke's arms tighten. "Elaborate."

"You made cameras?" I look at Ollie, and every one of the guys groan.

"I sure did, babe. Want to check out my set

up?" The room goes so silent you could easily hear a pin drop on the floor above us.

"Shit. He won't even let me into his bat cave," Creed stage whispers and I widen my eyes, but Ollie looks at him like he's bored.

"Because you can't keep your hands to yourself, and you'll end up breaking shit."

"You won't let anyone down there," Lukas points out.

"She's different."

I smile. "I'd love to see it."

Lukas grunts. "What shady fuck?" He turns us toward Mathias.

It's an odd name that actually suits him, but I don't like it. Too formal.

"Can I call you, Matty? Actually, I'm not asking. That's your name from me now." I get an oddly strange look from him as Lukas tenses underneath me before Matty shrugs.

"Whatever. There's been a new guy in town this past week. Showed up the day after the Halloween party and has been following you guys as well as thing one and thing two over there whenever they're on campus."

"Someone's following me? Someone that isn't

you weirdos?" I squeak, feeling sick to my stomach. I knew it.

I knew I could feel more eyes on me, I just hoped it was them upping their spying since we officially met.

"Yep." Matty nods.

"Who?" Lukas is pissed.

"We don't have a name yet, but I've seen him with that FBI prick a few times."

I sigh, some of the tension leaving me.

"Could he be working with Daniels?" I ask, and Ollie is the one to answer.

"Don't know that yet, babe, but I'm working on it."

I stare at him for a long moment before giving him a sharp nod.

"Everyone needs to act like nothing has changed. We need to go on like we don't know he's watching," Matty says and I nod, knowing I can do that.

"Any chance he's after us, and Haliee is just an innocent in this?" Corden questions.

Now I'm confused. "Why would anyone be after you?" I ask, and everyone stares at Luke.

"You haven't told her?" I hear Corden ask.

"I started to on Halloween, then everything went to shit."

Standing up, I turn to him, my back to the rest of the room. "Tell me what?"

He bites his lip, looking nervous. "Remember when we watched *Boondock Saints* and had that conversation about good and bad and all the grey in between?"

I squint at him. "Yes."

Of course, I remember, it's my favourite movie and I told him anyone that fought and killed for the greater good was alright by me.

My past with Dimitri has clearly warped my brain a little, but whatever.

"She watches the Saints?" I hear Creed mutter, and fight the smirk.

"What if I told you that we operate on the dark side of the line? But, like them, we only punish or kill a certain group of people."

I blink. Is he joking? He's joking, right? He has to be.

There's no way these guys could get away with vigilante killing. But Halloween…Creed said…

"You're murderers?" I whisper, and Lukas winces.

"Only of men who beat, rape, and kill women and children."

Oh, my fucking heart. "You give them the voice the law doesn't," I state matter of factly, and he nods.

"We do."

I take a deep breath, fighting the panic inside me that wants to be afraid. It's a normal human reaction to hear "murder" and run, but I'm not normal.

"Okay then," I sigh and sit back in his lap.

"That's it?" The other guys all say in unison, and I shrug.

"Are you going to kill me or my dad?" They blink and shake their heads no. "Then yeah, that's it. You give people a voice like I never got to have. I can't hate you for that."

"Holy fucking shit. Marry me." Creed falls to his knees, and I laugh, the tension breaking around us.

"Not a fucking chance, asshole. Sit down." I motion him back to his seat, and he pouts the entire way there.

"You're really not mad?" Luke leans in to whisper in my ear, and I shake my head.

"I'm not mad. Not sure how I'm going to tell Dad I'm dating a killer, but I'm not mad."

He chuckles as he pulls back. "Your Dad knows I'm not, and these are his words, 'completely on the right side of the law'."

Now that surprises me. "You told him but not me?!"

"Not completely. I just wanted him to know you were safe no matter where you went."

I growl. "You both suck." Now I'm the one pouting, and everyone laughs.

"Back on track," Matty pipes in. "We don't know who he is, but we aren't taking any chances. Keep your eyes open, always have a weapon, and don't act suspicious."

We spend the rest of the afternoon coming up with different plans for different possible scenarios with this stranger involved, and I go home feeling safer than I've ever felt in my life.

Lukas
Chapter Nineteen

Now that the shady fucker has been brought to our attention, I see him everywhere.

I don't have a good enough excuse as to why I didn't see him beforehand, but I know why.

I was wrapped up in my girl too hard to notice anything because she's my fucking everything.

I'm trying really hard not to hate myself too much over it, though, because I knew my brothers had our backs. I knew that Haliee was safe because they wouldn't allow her to be anything else.

Doesn't stop my Pride from getting the best of me from time to time.

More than anything, I want to walk up to the slimy fuck and strangle him until he tells us all of his secrets, but Mathias is right. We need to play this down like we aren't onto him.

"Luke, you really need to relax, baby." Haliee grips my hand harder, and I sigh.

"It's hard for me to admit I'm an idiot, Scratch." She narrows her eyes at me before dragging me into a break between buildings, shoving my back against a wall.

"I'd like to think you were just really into me to the point of being distracted."

I smirk at her as she leans into me, my hands resting on her lower back. "Scratch, you are the only thing that makes me lose sense of my job." She stiffens and I curse. "Not what I meant. I just mean, you're so hot that I'm literally always hard and wanting you."

"Are you saying you're just so preoccupied with wanting to fuck me that you can't think straight?" She smirks and I groan, my dick thickening at her sass. It never stops wanting to be inside of her, and it's fucking annoying.

Sort of. Okay, it's not. She feels like nirvana.

"Yeah, Scratch, that's exactly what I'm saying."

She bites her lip as a blush creeps into her cheeks. "Would it make you feel better to know that

I'm one hundred percent dick drunk when it comes to you?"

I bark out a laugh and pull her closer. "Baby, that makes me feel a million times better."

"Good. Then stop being an idiot and just go with it. I love you Lukas, and I'm flattered you get distracted. Besides, I know we both missed the obvious, but I also know that you would have easily killed them before they could lay a hand on me."

I nod, kissing her head. "Without a second thought."

She smiles up at me. "And I'm not one hundred percent helpless either, you know." She winks and I laugh again, pulling her back out onto the walkway.

"Trust me, Scratch, I will never forget how hot you looked standing over that fucker. Or the fact that you took on Creed. You're so fucking perfect," I groan, and she giggles.

"Noted. Violence turns you on."

I shake my head. "No, you being able to defend yourself is what turns me on. It's hot as hell to watch you wield a knife like it's an extension of your arm."

She gives me this sexy smile and leans into me.

"I'm glad my slight deviance turns you on because I'm so wet right now."

Fuck, she's going to kill me. "Haliee, we have class," I groan and she sighs.

"Can't we sit in the back and have some naughty play time? It's on my list of fantasies."

Ah, hell. "Woman, you're going to fucking kill me."

She beams as we walk into our next class. "I'll take that as a yes."

I'm so fucking screwed for this girl.

Corden

I WATCH a giggling Haliee and a smirk wearing Lukas enter into the classroom like some sick rom-com playing out in real time, and it's irritating.

Not because I'm not happy for my brother, but I want her too. She's like this perfect mix of sweet and innocent with a dash of badass.

Fuck, I need my dick sucked badly, but every single time I approach a cock target, little Cordy shrivels up into turtle shell mode.

Amber has been really persistent on wanting my

dick back in her, too, but I've already told her to fuck off in more ways than I should have to.

Even the thought of being with her again makes me sick to my stomach, and little Cordy is one hundred percent not on board with sticking it in any of those bitches ever the fuck again.

Actually, it seems Haliee is the only one I get hard for anymore.

Well, the only woman anyway.

I keep my eyes locked on Haliee as they move up the steps together toward the back of the room, and from my angle in the corner I have an open view to everything and everyone, even under the desks.

A strategic move Barren and I discussed after the first day of class.

The professor finally busts into the room looking frazzled and unkept like he didn't get to shower and change after sleeping in yesterday's clothes or some shit.

Gross.

Barren huffs out a breath and fiddles with his bracelet to help get his stress and anxiety under control.

Swinging my eyes back toward the happy couple, I see her look at Luke with stars in her eyes.

I feel both little Cordy and my heart responding to that look.

I want her eyes on me like that.

Lukas leans over to whisper in her ear, and places his hand on her thigh squeezing it a bit. The professor yammers away ignorant as ever to anything the students are up to in the room.

All eyes are on him except mine.

They are firmly locked on Lukas' hand traveling up Haliee's leg. I watch her tiny inhale, and half feel the breath she releases from here.

Damn, I wish that was me.

Lukas keeps whispering in her ear as his hand makes contact with the sweetest part of her body, making my dick press painfully against my pants.

I envy him. I'd love to be the one close enough to touch her. To feel and hear the short intakes of breath she makes as her chest rises and falls with the movement of his hand between her thighs.

Haliee puts her head down on Lukas' shoulder to stifle her moans, but somehow, I feel them. I feel them so deep in my soul I might cum in my jeans just from watching her rush toward release.

I watch as Lukas picks up his pace, knowing her body enough to get her to the orgasm she's so clearly chasing.

I couldn't look away from this if I tried.

Just as I feel myself about to explode, she squeezes her thighs together, grabbing his shirt in a death grip, signalling her release.

Lukas gives her a minute to come down and draws his hand back, taking those same fingers into his mouth.

Fuck my life. I'm jealous of Lukas' fucking fingers now? That's some fucked up shit.

Haliee composes herself as best she can, but she must feel eyes on her because she cuts her gaze my way.

I put on a huge smile and wink at her for good measure when she does something that cuts me for a loop.

She flips me off and smiles back. Lukas looks ready to murder me, so I give him a finger gun for good measure cause if I'm going out, I'm going out like a badass.

This girl is going to be the death of me. I feel it.

A sharp jab hits my arm and I swing a glare at my twin.

"Pay attention to the fucking teacher and stop drawing attention to her. Go get fucking laid after class and get your head back in the game." Snarky bastard.

"No one fucking appeases me lately. I'm not touching anyone else right now. My head is firmly in place, brother," I snarl back, keeping my voice low.

Barren sucks in a sharp breath, looking at me like I've grown an extra head.

I get it. Fucking is my forte. I'm not Lust for nothing.

"Maybe I'll hit up Ollie once we get home," I murmur under my breath, deflating a bit.

Barren is still looking at me like I need to be committed, so I swing my gaze back toward Haliee.

Her face is etched in a deep frown as she watches us. I give her a reassuring smile and turn back toward professor dumbass.

I'll definitely hit up Ollie when I get home. Creed can just fuck right off.

Me:

Be ready for me when I get home, Ollie. I need you right now.

Haliee

I'M NOT EXACTLY sure how I went from completely inexperienced, to letting my sinfully sexy boyfriend get me off in the back of a classroom, but I'm here for it.

That was one of the hottest experiences of my life. I don't even care that Corden started watching at some point. It added a type of forbidden feeling to it. Even Luke didn't seem to be too bothered by it.

"Why are we going to your house again?" I ask him as we're pulling into his driveway.

"Mathias needs to talk to me about something that he doesn't want to say over the phone." He's grumbling because he wanted to take me home and have his wicked way with me, and now that's been delayed. I can't help but laugh at the stern pout he's sporting.

"Aww, baby, don't worry. You can thoroughly fuck me when we get home." I wink, jumping out of the car before he can grab me.

He joins me outside the car and grabs my hand, pulling me against him.

"Oh, Scratch, you should know I'm not waiting until we get home to be inside your sweetness." I shiver and he smirks, squeezing my ass before drawing me inside the house.

"Good, you're here." Matty looks between us and rolls his eyes. "Ten minutes, man. I need you to control your dick for ten minutes." Lukas grumbles but leaves with him, and I make my way into the living room before seeing Creed.

"My Doll!" He jumps up, and it's my turn to be the one rolling my eyes.

"Not a Doll, Creed."

He tilts his head. If he were a puppy, it would be cute, but the action just makes him look like a psychotic serial killer. Huh. I guess that makes sense. "But you're so perfect and beautiful. I bet you bleed so pretty."

I snort, shaking my head at him. "That's the most fucked up shit you've ever said to me."

He shrugs. "It's not like you're afraid of me."

I narrow my eyes at the glee on his face. "I stabbed you, Creed. I'll do it again, but next time I'll make it hurt."

He moans, adjusting his dick. "Promise?"

Why the fuck am I not afraid of him? I should be running in the opposite direction.

I'm about to spew some bullshit at him when I hear something that sounds a lot like someone fighting.

"What the fuck is that?" I start to move toward the back of the house, and Creed stands up.

"It's nothing, Doll. I wouldn't…" He trails off when I give him a nasty look, holding his hands up with a smile.

Creepy fuck.

I follow where the sounds are coming from before knocking, but no one answers. The second I hear a pained groan, I open the door and freeze.

Holy shit. Ummm….

What…? I really should turn-

"Oh, God, Cord, yes." Oliver is sweating and panting as a very sweaty and hot Corden pounds into his ass, and the sight has me so frazzled. I let out a gasp as Creed steps in behind me.

"You like taking this dick, Ollie?" Corden slaps

his ass, moving his eyes to meet mine, and I lick my lips.

"Fuck, yes. Harder."

Oh fuck. I'm so turned on right now I can't even think. My panties are drenched so much I'm pretty sure it would show if my jeans weren't black.

"Look at our audience, Ollie." His head snaps up like he didn't realize we were here. As his eyes connect with mine, I see them widen for a split second before he lets out a guttural moan.

I flinch when I feel hands against my bare stomach, but lean into the person behind me.

"It's hot, isn't it, Doll? Watching Corden fuck him?" I swallow, nodding and he chuckles into my neck.

"Are you wet for us, Haliee?" I moan, leaning harder into him and rubbing my thighs together. Fuck, I'm so turned on.

"See our girl, Ollie? See what the sight of us together does for her?" Corden's eyes never move from mine, and it's one of the hottest things I've ever seen.

"Ours," Ollie pants, and Creed's hands travel further under my shirt, just barely connecting with my breasts, then moving back across my stomach.

"You're ours, right, Doll?" Creed uses his nails to drag across my skin, making me whimper.

"Shit," I hiss out, my eyes moving from Corden's to watch where he's thrusting in and out of Oliver. "Doesn't that...hurt?" I whisper, and both Corden and Creed laugh.

"Does this hurt you, Ollie?" Corden pulls out before slamming back into him hard enough his body juts forward.

"Oh, fuck, no," he moans, reaching down to wrap his hand around his own dick.

"You going to cum for us, Ollie? Show our girl just how hot you are when you feel me?"

He moans, nodding his head as his hand jerks faster, and Creed kisses my neck.

Oh, holy fuck.

"Are you going to cum from just watching, Haliee? Or do you need some help?"

I whimper, spreading my legs a little and he chuckles, his hand moving lower. "Please," I beg, and he gently bites my neck as Corden curses, his hips moving faster in and out of Ollie's ass as he watches us.

"My pleasure, Doll." Creed's hand unbuttons my jeans before slipping in past my panties. Connecting with my slickness, he moans.

"How wet is she?" Corden rasps, and Creed groans against my ear.

"She's so wet I can barely get my finger to stay on her clit. Her panties are drenched."

I moan when his finger slides through my folds before slipping into my core. "Yes. Oh, God." I'm so close already, and he knows it.

"That's it, Doll. You're already squeezing me so tight. Are you guys going to cum together?" He lifts his head to look up at the two fucking in front of us and I throw my head back, screaming my release as his finger thrusts into me a couple more times, his palm connecting with my clit.

"Fucking, fuck!" Corden slams into Ollie, screaming his release as Ollie lets go of his as well, his cum spraying all over his hand and the sheet below them.

I'm frozen in time, the pleasure still travelling through my body as Corden and Ollie crumble to the bed, their breaths coming hard and fast when a voice seeps into my brain.

"What the fuck?" Lukas walks in past Creed and I, his hand still inside my pants, and I blush. "Haliee?" He doesn't look upset, but I feel sick.

"Luke," I gasp, pushing myself away from Creed, his hand sliding from me.

"Was it consensual?" He looks to me before Corden laughs, drawing his attention to the pile of hot guys on the bed. He blinks looking back to me, and I blush.

"Uh, yeah."

He smirks a little. "Got a little too hot watching them, did you?"

Oh, fuck, swallow me whole.

"Yep," I squeak, and they all laugh. He pulls me to him, gripping my chin in his hand.

"It's okay, Scratch. I love you, and I love them. If you want to be with them, I will be okay with it as long as it's only us."

Wait…huh? "I'm not having sex with them!" I shriek and he smiles.

"Not yet, but if and when you do, just know I will be okay with it."

I frown, unsure how I feel about that. "You don't want me to yourself?"

He frowns at me. "I do. I fucking love you, baby, and I've never loved anyone." He sighs, bringing his forehead to mine. "But you're the best thing to ever happen to me. You bring me light and happiness. I won't stop you from doing the same for them if it's what you want."

My eyes start to tear up. "I love you so much,

Lukas. But I'm not…I'm not ready to be with anyone but you right now." I look around the room. "Not for actual sex, anyway." They all nod in understanding as another sound of footsteps approach.

"Seriously? It smells like a fucking orgy in here!" Matty barks, breaking up the seriousness of the moment, and I laugh.

"Jealous, Matty?" I wink, walking past him with his mouth gaping open. "Lukas, I want to go do what you promised me outside."

He chuckles, slapping Matty on the back. "You got it, Scratch. See you guys later!" he hollers back.

The last thing I hear before we walk out the door is Creed commanding Ollie to suck, and I'm completely ready to go again just picturing that.

It's going to be a long night of sexiness ahead!

Oliver
Chapter Twenty

"I'm watching you, you slippery fuck," I tell the screens in my bat cave.

I've been watching this prick for a few weeks now, and his tailing of Lukas and Haliee is ramping up to the point Creed and I had to sneak cameras all around her house and into the forest just to make sure we truly had eyes everywhere.

I still haven't gotten an ID on him and that's never a good thing. He's either in deep undercover with the FBI and his entire identity has been erased, or he's a ghost.

If he's a ghost, I can only assume he's working for that Russian prick that's after our Angel.

The weather has changed so much, and the

snow has started falling in fat flakes, making this task that much more difficult. The trails are becoming thick, but we always prepare for that with the winter gear we stock up on.

We're lucky that the roads aren't as steep here, so plows come through and keep them clear. But even then, ice is an issue.

I wonder if Haliee would like to make snow angels with me?

I can still feel her eyes on me as Cord plowed into me from behind, and how turned on she'd been.

Fuck, I'll never get that look out of my head.

She's been a little distant with us since then, staying close to Lukas. That'll change soon, though. She's just not used to the positive attention she receives from us.

I also assume she's trying to wrap her head around the desire for more than one man. It's not a normal thing really, but I mean…chicks read those reverse harem things all the time, so it's not unheard of.

Though, seven of us might be a lot for the poor girl considering we're all crazy.

I twist my chair around and spot the black roses I got her.

She didn't even notice the first one I got her when she got that ugly as balls cat, but it's ok. I'll just start leaving them in places she'll have to see them.

Twisting back around, I lock my gaze on her bedroom camera. I know Creed and I will catch shit over that and I'm really not trying to play Peeping Tom, but she needs to be kept safe, and this is the only way we know how.

She's just come back from the shower, so she's clean, happy, and bright-eyed. Watching her dance around the room as she gets ready has me smiling a little.

She's just too gorgeous.

Lukas is in the living room chatting up her Dad, and I can tell by Brent's body language something is off.

I really need to get audio on this shit. I snap my head over toward the camera that points at the driveway as a car rolls up.

It's one I haven't seen before, so I quickly shoot off a text to Lukas and watch him check his phone, excusing himself to the door.

Detective Daniels hops out the slick SUV and my blood pressure rises. Haliee's still dancing around her room, and Brent looks close to running.

Something's up. I feel it in my soul.

I don't think. I just act, and I really hope Haliee forgives me for this.

I quickly start typing in codes and link the necklace that Lukas gave her to my system, activating the tracker on it.

He doesn't know I even had access to it to embed a tiny tracker, but I do it with everyone I love. Just in case.

I promised myself I would never use it because it meant taking away that small bit of freedom she's gained since showing up here, but I can't shake the sinking feeling in my gut.

I'm turning it on for her safety. If she's ever taken, we need to know where the fuck she is because the seven of us will burn the world to the ground to get her back.

Lukas looks about ready to kill as him and Daniels exchange words. I don't know what's up but whatever it is has Lukas close to unleashing his demon.

Daniels nods and hops back in his car, driving off and leaving Lukas to stare after him.

I watch Lukas take his phone out and the group chat immediately pings.

· · ·

Lukas:

Code Angel. Meeting at the house in fifteen.

Fuck! This is not good.

Lukas

"Luke, I really need you to calm the fuck down and tell me what's going on," Haliee says from the passenger seat.

I can't think right now. My demon is too close to the edge, and I'm about to make a rash decision that will destroy everything we've built here.

If I kill Daniels and leave his body for the little

winter scavengers to pick apart, I won't get away with it because he's a federal fucking agent.

I careen into the driveway of my house and slam the brakes, jolting Haliee.

"FUCK!" Punching the steering wheel while Haliee trembles beside me, I see the door open and Ollie flying out the house. He snatches Haliee out of the car, looking at me with murder clear in his eyes.

"I know some shit went down and you're on edge, but if you ever, and I mean EVER, scare her like this again, I'll fucking end you, BROTHER!" he roars out before taking Haliee in the house.

They don't get it. How would they? I haven't explained shit yet.

A fucking shift change. Daniels said we will be enforcing a shift change, meaning I will be ripped from her side, and HE will be watching her.

Over. My. Dead. Fucking. Body.

My hands are tied, though.

If I refuse, I can be removed from her case immediately and that further muddles the waters.

Creed comes out the house looking like a raging bull as he yanks open my door. Without saying a word, he just points toward the woods, and I know what he wants.

He wants a fight. I need it to release some of this anger flowing through me, and Creed is the perfect escape. He gets off on the pain, and I owe him a few punches for touching Haliee before he was given permission.

We head deep into the woods, tracking through snow, and I remove my shirt to let the bite of the bitter cold seep deep into my bones and fuel me.

Creed still has his back turned on me, but if the heaving in his shoulders is anything to go by, he's equally as pissed as I am.

"One request. No visible injuries. My Doll isn't ready for that kind of violence yet," Creed snarls out, shocking the ever living fuck out of me.

"What the fuck is happening to us?" I whisper more to myself than anything, not really expecting a response.

"She happened. We were damned spirits. Bound and chained to dole out the work of the devil, never feeling any kind of light or love. Then heaven took mercy on our broken souls and sent us a piece of their world. I'm done waiting for you to wake up and realize she's meant to fix us all. You've been selfish, Pride. Today, you're going to take a fucking hit," Creed says before he turns around, launching at me.

I'm ready, though. We slam to the ground in a tangle of brutal fists and snarls. I take two shots to his ribs before he goes for my fucking kidneys.

I can already tell I'll be pissing blood for the next week.

I feel my knuckles bust open on the next hit I land to the centre of Creed's stomach, but the motherfucker is built like a brick wall and just huffs out a laugh like a psycho.

"You think you can keep her to yourself and that the rest of us can never have her. You're wrong. Your jealously has you bested today!" Creed roars out, launching at me again.

Hold the goddamn phone. He thinks I'm pissed over sharing her?

I catch his fist before it collides with my chest and twist it behind his back, bringing his back to my front.

"This has nothing to do with jealously, brother. Detective dick showed up at Haliee's an hour ago and laid down the order for a fucking shift change. I have no choice but to comply or I will lose my position in this case and possibly lose my job. Period." I get the words out through gritted teeth as my soul still rages.

"And you think you're the only one that can

protect her? Have you completely lost the last brain cells in your dumbass head? They may remove you from her side, but they can't do a damn thing about us being there, you fucking asshole!" Creed growls back.

All the fight leaves me instantly and I drop back from Creed. I deserve whatever hits he has coming at me. For the first time since we came to live here, my brothers weren't even a thought in my mind when it came to this situation.

I fucking doubted them.

I drop to my knees in the snow, letting the bitterness of winter swallow me in its icy embrace.

Creed stands over me with a sneer on his face, shocking me yet again when he puts his hand out to help me up.

"Get fucking dressed. We have plans to lay out to make sure my Doll has the demons she summoned at her beck and call."

We clean up in the snow to the best of our abilities, trying to hide what damage we've done, and make our way back to the house.

Stepping inside, the breath leaves my lungs when I see Haliee curled up in Ollie's lap still trembling from my anger earlier. I take a step toward her, and she flinches back.

The pain that sears my soul makes me want to fucking die right there.

I did that to her. I made her fear me after I fucking promised her she would never have to be afraid of me.

I can only drop my head in defeat because, just as I thought I had the girl of my dreams, I may have fucking lost her.

Torren

God, he looks fucking broken. He really is head over heels in love with her.

I watch his face fall as he takes in the sight of Haliee shaking in Ollie's arms, and I feel for him. He slowly walks to Haliee, and when she flinches back, it's powerful enough to knock him down.

"Haliee, baby," he speaks softly, kneeling in front of them. Ollie is watching him with narrowed eyes, and I have no idea where the fuck this is going to go, but we're all watching.

Waiting.

"I didn't mean to scare you." His voice breaks and she looks over to him. "Daniels implemented a shift change and I was so fucking scared because he's *forcing* me to leave your side once in a while." He blinks before her face turns angry.

"He WHAT?! He can't do that!" She jolts upright in Ollie's arms.

"He can, Scratch. If I don't comply with leaving your house, boyfriend or not, he will remove me from your case completely and I could lose my job."

She lets out a growl of her own, and Ollie speaks. "He can't keep all of us away from her."

Lukas sighs and nods. "I realize that now, but I wasn't thinking. The only thought was he was forcing me away from my girl. Our girl, and I couldn't do shit."

Haliee jumps into Lukas' arms, kissing him hard and squeezing his neck. "I don't trust him, Lukas. I hate him so much." She sobs into his neck, and he holds her tight.

He said our girl.

Holy shit, he's going to share her with us.

"I know, baby. Your Dad and I are working on it." He shares a look with Ollie before looking at each one of us. "I didn't mean to exclude you guys in this, I just got so angry and wasn't thinking. Brent will be fine with one of us always staying with her."

We all grunt in agreement.

"If he's shady like I think he is, he's going to fight us on it." I nod in agreement with Mathias.

"Matt's right. There's going to be some head-butting that goes down. I don't understand why he seems to want to leave her alone." It doesn't sit right with me at all.

"He wants to insert another agent in my place." We all growl.

"Not fucking happening! No one is sharing my room unless it's you guys. I don't trust him or anyone else," Haliee states, and we all smile proudly at her fire.

"I know, Scratch. We won't let it happen, baby."

She nods, kissing him and curling into his lap. "Thank you," she whispers and Ollie pets her head while Creed moves to Luke's side.

"Doll, we will never let anything happen to you. We're your demons and we will kill anyone who tries to touch you."

She snorts but smiles at the psycho. "That should scare me, but it doesn't." Shit, I think she's into his crazy.

He smiles at her. "My Doll likes my darkness."

She shivers. "As long as it's not aimed at me like it was in the classroom."

He scowls. "I'm sorry, Doll. That was bad."

Luke snorts. "You fucking think?" He shakes his head at Creed.

"So, what are we going to do?" I ask, and Mathias is the one to stand up.

"We plan a schedule. She is never without at least one of us by her side and one of us watching from a distance that they can't see."

"Aww, Matty. You make it sound like you actually care," she taunts him, and his eyes narrow.

"Angel, watch it."

She chuckles, and he shakes his head, a look of confusion in his eyes.

He has no clue what to do with his feelings for her and it's kind of hilarious.

"Matt looks like he's about to have an aneurysm," I hear Corden whisper to Barren who slaps him on the back of the head.

"Shut up, idiot. Now isn't the time for jokes."

Cord sighs. "Sorry, was just trying to lighten the somber mood."

Haliee looks at Cord and lifts an eyebrow. "You realize this prick is trying to get me alone to most likely kidnap me, right?"

Cord blinks then scowls. "You really think that?"

She nods. "I haven't trusted him since the day I

met him, and he's proven he can't be trusted with all the shit he's been pulling with Luke." She shrugs. "Dimitri doesn't want me dead, so kidnapping is the only possible choice."

He curses. "Sorry, Hal."

She gives him a sad smile. "It's okay. Let's just all come up with a plan then set up a meeting."

She pulls out her phone and calls Brent on some sort of private line they've set up that can't be traced, and we spend a good hour talking about what to do.

It will take time, but this fucker is going down. He *will* be added to our kill list if he's crooked.

Haliee
Chapter Twenty-One

"You sure that you're okay with this, Dad?" I turn to face him on the couch while the guys all watch on through a hidden camera. It's still one of Ollie's, but there's also a few hidden microphones to capture the sound so they hear every word.

Apparently, he's having trouble getting sound into his untraceable inventions.

Lukas is the only one actually sitting in the room with us, and Ollie has given him some sort of jammer to stop them from discretely checking the room for bugs.

My sweet Ollie is a genius and it's kinda hot.

"Yeah, Sparrow. I just need you safe." I smile at

him. "I trust Lukas, and if he trusts these brothers of his, then that's all that matters."

I nod, giving him a hug while there's a knock at the door. "Thank you, Eagle."

He pulls me in close, his eye level with the camera. "Door is never closed when it's anyone other than Lukas."

I shake my head, smiling at him. Just thinking about the reactions on the other side of the camera has me ready to giggle. "Promise."

He nods as Daniels stomps into the room with the guy who has been following us recently.

"What the hell is the meaning of this?!" His face is red, and I lift an eyebrow at him.

We all discussed it and decided I would be the one to stand my ground with him. He needs to see me as a grown woman and not a kid, and he's about to learn I'm very capable of fighting my own battles. And winning them.

"I'm not happy about this shift change."

He narrows his eyes at me. "It's not up to you." Dad stiffens beside me, but I pat his knee to keep him from saying anything.

"I beg to differ. I'm eighteen years old and fully capable of being made aware of the decision made on my behalf."

He looks at me in disbelief while the strange guy smirks. I already hate him.

"You're joking," Daniels fumes.

I shake my head. "I'm not. If you insist on separating Lukas and I from time to time, and it will be very few and far between, then I will be having some other friends stay with me on those nights."

He takes a few steps toward me, but the stranger holds him back.

"Who are these people? We need to do background checks on them to make sure your safety is taken seriously," the new stranger says, and I fight to not roll my eyes at the bullshit he's spewing.

"They're trusted friends of *my boyfriend*, and Dad and I both trust them enough to have them in our house. That isn't a decision we take lightly."

Daniels looks about ready to blow a blood vessel. "You can't just tell me how your protection is to be laid out. That's not how Witness Protection works."

I nod in understanding, standing up to face him down. "I'm not. You can have whatever *agent* you choose in here, but I will not let my father and I be left alone with another person in this house that we don't know. You may not know what it's like to be targeted by a sick monster, but I do. We both do, and I will not budge on this." I stand up even straighter, moving closer to him. "You can control the agents and protection around me all you want, but who I choose to have here for a sleepover is none of your business. Are we clear?"

He looks like he wants to say something, but the stranger clears his throat and nods to Daniels, making him cool down.

"Fine. Have it your way, but the second they screw up, they're out of here," he spits out.

I nod, conceding to his rule because I know for a fact they won't screw up and risk my safety.

Well, Creed might because he's psychotic, but I have a feeling Ollie will be here to keep him settled on the nights he's here.

"Thank you, Agent Daniels. It was nice talking to you."

He growls a little before they say their goodbyes and stomp out of the house, not looking back as they drive off in their shiny SUV.

"Damn, Sparrow. I'm so proud of you right now. My little girl is all grown up," Dad's voice breaks, and I sigh.

"I grew up a long time ago, Dad."

He nods, swallowing. "I know, sweetheart. I know."

"Scratch, that was impressive as hell. Did anyone notice that they didn't even look my way the entire time they were here?" Lukas questions, and Dad nods.

"Yeah. None of this is sitting right with me. You all need to be on your guard and protect my little girl."

"And you, Dad. I won't survive losing you."

He sighs, nodding. "Yeah, Sparrow. And me."

"Promise me you'll be just as careful, Dad."

He smiles down at me. "I'm always careful, sweetheart. I promise."

"Thank you. Now, can we go out to eat please? I'm craving a burger from the diner we first ate at."

They both chuckle at me but don't argue.

I HATE DANIELS.

I hate him with a passion I usually keep for my

mother and Dimitri, but this fucker was butt-hurt about me overruling him with *my* rights, and he decided to throw his weight around. He chose tonight to take Lukas away, right after we got back from the diner.

Joke is on him, though.

What? He thought we wouldn't have a plan already in place in case he threw his authority around? We weren't born yesterday.

Lukas is seething at the door as he lets the stranger stalker asshole into the house.

"Haliee, I'm sorry for the short notice. I hope it's alright that I'm here."

I shrug, knowing Mathias is already up in my room with Hope. "I don't like that you guys are forcing my boyfriend away but there's not much I can do about it. Is there?" I lift an eyebrow and he ignores me, scanning the room.

"Your father is at work?" he asks me, but he already knows the answer.

"Yeah, he is."

He looks to Lukas before turning back to me. "I'm Sergei Patrov." He holds out his hand, but I just narrow my eyes and tilt my chin.

Of course, the new guy has a Russian name. I

bet he's expecting a response of fear from me. He won't get it.

If he does work for Dimitri, he's not going to see my fear.

He must realize I'm not going to shake his hand because he sighs and drops it back to his side.

"Officer Michaels, you can go now. I'll keep your girl safe."

Lukas' eyes narrow, and I can tell it's taking everything for him to hold it together right now, so I walk over and wrap my arms around his waist.

"I'm okay," I assure him as his arms close around me in a tight hug. "Don't get yourself in trouble, babe."

He sighs, leaning down to kiss me gently. "Facetime me later, alright?"

I smile and nod, standing on my toes to kiss him more fully just to make Sergei uncomfortable. And to just kiss my man because I can. "I promise. I love you."

He swallows, eyeing his replacement protection. "Anything happens to her, and I promise I will destroy you," Lukas threatens, and I roll my eyes. I'm playing it cool on the outside, but damn does that possessiveness just do it for me.

"Nothing will." He turns to me. "I'm sorry it's

such short notice and you couldn't have a friend over, but you will be safe."

I lift an eyebrow as said friend makes his presence known in the living room. Agent Patrov's eyes widen in surprise, and I have to hold back the smile wanting to grace my lips.

Matty is a big boy, and the look currently on his face is dangerous.

"Not true, actually. This is Matty. Well, you better call him Mathias. I think I'm the only one on planet earth that can get away with calling him Matty."

Matty grunts and narrows his eyes before opening his one arm, beckoning me to come to his side, and I do.

It's something we all agreed on. I would be in physical contact with the guy guarding me before the other one leaves. That way it eliminates the chances of someone grabbing me for any reason, even if there is only two feet between them and I.

Always physically touching.

"Right. I wasn't aware we had anyone else in the house with us." Agent Petrov looks slightly pissed, but if they think that getting a hold of me is going to be easy, they've finally met their match.

"Someone will always be by her side." Matty

holds me tightly against him, and I see Lukas' shoulders relax.

"Okay, baby, I'm going to head out."

He walks over and kisses me lightly once more before standing and heading to the door. My heart aches to go with him, but for now we will play Daniels' game and see what he has up his sleeve.

"Love you."

He smiles at me. "Love you too, Scratch." Him and Matty share a look and then he's closing the door, walking away for the time being.

"Anyway, I think I'm going to go upstairs and work on my assignment." I take a slight step away from Matty, but he knows I'm not walking away from him. "You're welcome to watch tv or something down here while you wait." He looks between Matty and I then nods, making his way to the couch.

"If you need anything, Haliee, just call me." I'm about to respond, but Matty turns me toward the stairs and looks back over his shoulder.

"She won't," is all he says before ushering me up to my room where Hope is already laying across my books on the bed.

"Thanks for this, Matty," I sigh and he grunts, tilting his head like he's assessing me.

"I know I'm not Luke, but you're safe, Haliee. I won't let anything happen to you."

I give him a small smile, nodding and climbing onto the bed before lifting Hope off my books and into my lap.

"Hey, sweet girl. I missed your fluffy face," I baby talk to her, and Matty chuckles.

"I'm glad you like her."

I blink up at him. It's an odd thing for him to say before it dawns on me. "Did you get her for me?" I ask, and he instantly blushes, coughing to clear his throat.

"Uh...yeah. Not a big deal." He coughs again and I chuckle, tears brimming my eyes.

"I disagree. She's my first pet, and I kind of love her. Squished ugly face and all." He snorts and shakes his head before pointing to my books. "Wait. Did you give me the rose too? I've seen a few more of them over the past several weeks, but I wasn't sure they were actually for me. Actually, I tried to ignore them, afraid they were some sort of gift from Dimitri." He opens his mouth to answer when my phone rings. "Why is Ollie calling me?" I question, hitting answer.

"Angel?" he barks, and I roll my eyes.

"Yes, Ollie. No one else is going to be answering

my phone. Is everything alright?"

"The black roses are from me. I didn't even think that they may frighten you, I just wanted some way to show you and Creed that I was alright with the two of you being together," he curses under his breath. "Creed knew they were from me right away, but I didn't think about you and I'm so sorry."

I actually smile. "It's okay. Now that I know they're from you, I don't mind them but...don't they signify death?" I suck in a breath, and he cackles.

"They can, but in this case, they represent Obsession. Creed was instantly obsessed with you the second he saw you."

I groan. "He's a fucking psycho."

Him and Matty both laugh.

"You bet your sweet bottom he is, Angel. Gotta go, talk later." And he hangs up the phone.

It wouldn't be until much later that I realized he even has my bedroom bugged, too.

Asshole.

Mathias takes up a seat in the corner of the room, and I sigh.

"You don't have to sleep there, you know. We can make a palette on the floor for you."

"I'm fine, sweetie. Turn a movie on and get

some sleep. I'm watching over you. Always," Matty replies with a wink.

The adrenaline from the past month catches up to me quickly and I put my books away, laying down to get some rest.

Before I know it, I'm asleep, feeling safe even without Luke here.

I WAKE up sometime later and notice two things in tandem.

One, I'm really warm, and two, there's someone in the bed with me.

"You were thrashing around in your sleep. I tried to wake you, but you were out cold," Mathias whispers, feeling me stiffen as his arm tightens around my waist.

"Go back to sleep, sweetie. I'm here," Mathias says, and I comply closing my eyes and drifting off.

Corden
Chapter Twenty-Two

A week has passed since that sketchy fuck insisted on the shift change, and he's managed to keep Lukas out of the house for the most part.

He's pissed about it, but the guys have all been taking shifts, so he knows she's safe with us.

It's my turn tonight, and I'm sweating fucking bullets over it.

Everyone knows while you sleep is when your demons have free range in your mind.

I glance back toward Haliee and Lukas at the back of the classroom.

She's been thrashing around in her sleep since that first night with Mathias.

We all held our breaths, worried to hell about her. When he crawled in the bed with her and held her like he did, it shocked us all to hell. Matty boy hates being touched, but after a few minutes his face eased into the most peaceful I have ever seen him. Like somehow this little woman was bringing him the peace we've all been longing for but didn't think we deserved.

Even Lukas was shocked silent over it.

Creed had demanded Ollie let him into the basement for extra eyes on our girl, but as usual, no one is allowed down there but Ollie. It's his hard limit.

He went out and stole us each some iPads so we could remotely switch between the monitors from each camera. We all ended up with a front row seat to the cuddle fest that took place.

I have no clue why he insists on stealing this shit when we have the money to do so, but it's his demon.

Greed likes to provide for us, and he sees spending that kind of money as taking away from us rather than providing, so stealing was the only logical choice in his mind.

It's a fucked-up logic, but the slick fuck never seems to get busted.

Each night since then, every single brother of mine has crawled in bed to hold her in the middle of the night when her nightmares try to take over, but there's one problem.

I don't cuddle. I fuck and duck.

That's my specialty. I feel like my own issues are going to end up fucking this entire thing up for everyone, and it's making me nervous.

The last thing I want is for Haliee to be wary of us.

The professor finally calls for the end of class and everyone starts gathering their belongings. As usual, me and Barren hang back to wait on Lukas and Haliee.

We all started walking together once we realized we were all being watched, so we figured fuck it. There's safety in numbers.

Our group makes its way toward the exit, but the second we step outside, the back of my neck pricks with awareness. I feel myself stiffen as I look around the place, trying to sus out the danger.

Students are milling about in the courtyard watching us exit, but no one seems suspicious until my eyes hit the centre of the courtyard.

Dead square in the middle of them all is Amber

and the bitch squad, backed by the football jocks all sneering at us.

Haliee's steps falter a bit as she presses into Lukas' side more.

"I think it's time we've have a chat. I've been patient, but my patience has run its course with you lot. One little whore moves here, and you all lose your minds over who the queen is, and I will not share my crown with anyone else," Amber hisses her venom at us. "You're going to leave this slut right now and come back to me. I'm done waiting," Amber says, taking a step toward me like she has a right to.

Before any of us can reply, a voice booms from behind us, causing all of us to freeze, and fear starts spreading like wildfire across the student body.

Fucking pussies.

"Is that right, Amber?" Creed says, stepping out from the shadows.

Amber takes an uneasy step back from us and starts to tremble a bit. The once solid line of jocks now looks like they'd love to be anywhere else but here.

No one ever wants to willing take on Wrath. Not if they want to live, so their loyalty to Amber is only going to go so far.

"Judging by the way you all are standing in this courtyard looking like the world's most pathetic army tells me, you've forgotten the monsters that lurk at night around here." Creed continues walking slowly but surely over toward us.

"So, tell me something right now, little sheep. Are you all ready to take on the big bad wolves? Are you all to the point of confidence that you can beat us?" Creed says with a psychotic smile, sticking his hands in the pockets of his jeans and rocking back on his heels. "Because guess what?" Amber looks nervous, but sneers at him.

"What?!" she snaps, and he looks at her like she's nothing, just pissing her off farther.

"She has control of our demons now." He nods toward Haliee with a wink before sneering at the crowd again. "If she says you need to die? Neither of us will question it. Your ability to keep breathing solely rests in her hands unless you push us too far."

Haliee giggles over his antics, and even Amber swings a fearful gaze toward her.

That snaps Creed out of his easygoing stance as he charges her. Nobody steps up to help her either.

"Don't you dare look at my Doll, you pathetic whiny bitch," Creed snarls in her face, causing her to fall to the ground.

Everyone watching jerks back in fear, recognizing the demon that has been unleashed amongst us.

Lukas nudges Haliee toward me, stalking over to Creed and Amber.

Amber's hateful gaze lands on me, and I can't help but to rub it in a little as I throw my arm around Haliee's waist, kissing her head, and she leans into me with complete trust.

It's in this moment I decide I'm going to share the pain of my past with her. I need her to understand why I have always been a closed off whore.

I don't want her to hate me because she doesn't understand…and I need her to see that it's only her now.

She's all I fucking see.

"It's not fair! You were all supposed to be mine!" Amber screeches out.

"Why the fuck would I touch a slimy ass bitch like you?" Creed snarls back. "You had Corden because he thought you were hot, but you never would have had the rest of us. You never would have kept him, either. You were a willing pussy for him to fuck when he was bored," Creed lays into her, and I pull Haliee tighter against me.

"It's okay," I whisper into her hair, and she relaxes again.

"What kind of delusional fucked up world are you living in, you stupid cunt?!" Creed keeps going. "And you fucked up and lost Corden when you decided to show how vile you truly are by wanting someone to drug and rape *our* girl."

Lukas walks up to defuse the situation, but it's too far gone.

I look down at Haliee and make a split second call.

"Think you can corral Creed back in his cage, cowgirl?" I whisper in her ear.

Haliee chuckles, pulling away from me, walking to Creed and placing a hand between his shoulder blades.

"Creed? I need you right now," she whispers.

Everyone sucks in a breath of shock and fear as Creed whips his glare down toward Haliee before smiling.

Deflating almost instantly, he takes her hand and just walks away.

"See, this is the bullshit we were talking about. You never had us and never will, Amber. Just fuck off," Lukas grinds out, following after them.

He's not going to leave her side until the absolute moment he's forced to.

Hell, he hasn't been sleeping well, either. They've gotten so used to being side by side, that they're both suffering from being pulled apart.

Barren's still looking around at the students lingering, and jumps at the closest of them, laughing as they trip over themselves to get away.

Amber's still on the ground glaring at me when I move my focus back on her.

"It seems I wasn't clear when I said this dick was locked down now. I mean, props to you for having the whole student body present to watch you get your ass dropped down there thing, but YOU. ARE. NOTHING! Now, fuck all the way off," I say patting her head like she's a little bitch for good measure.

She shrieks and launches to her feet, growling at me before stomping off with her bitch squad and jock boys trailing behind her.

"Corden, let's roll!" Barren yells out. I turn and stalk off after them.

Later that night, I'm pacing around Haliee's room while her and that fucking cat stare at me, watching my every move.

My phone keeps vibrating in my pocket. I just know it's the guys telling me to chill the fuck out, but I can't.

I really fucking can't.

I'm about to climb into bed with this girl, and even though Lukas has said she's ours, I know for a fact she doesn't want me…at least not yet. I can't exactly blame her. All she's ever heard or seen is that I'm a whore, and it's going to take a lot of work to have her see past that.

I haven't been laid in weeks aside from blowing off some steam with Ollie, and as much as I like being with him, he doesn't compare to the feeling of a soft, wet pussy swallowing my dick. He just doesn't.

Fuck.

"Uh, Corden. Could you maybe sit down?" Haliee raises an eyebrow at me, and I stop to stare at her.

"I don't know."

"You don't know if you can sit down?"

I sigh. "I don't know if I can stay here," I squeak out, and her face falls. "Shit. It's not like that. I just…you know I'm addicted to sex, right?"

She stares me down, nodding. "Kind of hard to miss, yeah."

I snort. "Sex keeps the nightmares from my past at bay," I try and explain.

She blinks, moving over to give me room on the bed, and I sit down. "I don't really know much about any of your pasts, but I won't judge you."

I give her a small smile.

"Never thought you would. You know that, aside from Luke, that we've all had pretty shit lives." She nods. "Well, Barren and I are no different. While I can't tell you his part of the story, I can say that, while our mother was essentially torturing him as a child, our father was busy doing shit to me. It was like they tag teamed to get us apart and cause maximum damage."

She makes a whimpering sound. "Cord."

I shake my head. "Please let me tell you? I think

it will help you understand why I seek physical attention as an escape." I scrunch my nose. "Or used to. I don't really want anyone aside from you anymore, so I'm kind of struggling."

She blinks at me, surprise evident in her eyes. "Uh…thank…you?"

I bark out a laugh and she smiles at me. Fuck, she really is perfect.

"Our parents were fucked, Haliee. Sort of like your mom, but in a different way." She sucks in a breath. "Again, I can't tell you what our mother did to Barren, but our father?" I shake my head to clear the haunting memories causing a flood of emotions. "He was a sadistic prick. A pedophile." I swallow, and she cries out.

I hold my arms open, seeing she wants to hold me, so I let her. As much for her comfort as my own.

It will be easier to get the story out if I don't have to look into her eyes.

"Is this okay?" she asks once she's curled into a ball on my lap, her arms wrapped around my waist and I sigh, squeezing her tight.

"It's more than okay." She nods. "Once Barren was busy and we couldn't fight together, he'd come for me. It started with small touches, caressing my hair and my back… but slowly it turned into more intimate touches, private areas that I knew weren't supposed to be touched. I was a kid, but I just knew, you know?" She sniffs, nodding. "When I was about eight, he started asking me to lick him. To pleasure him and get him off while he touched me. I didn't like it, but I didn't want to anger him, either. He was my dad and I just wanted him to be proud of me."

She sucks in a breath, her body stiff in my lap. "I'm sorry," she cries softly, and I squeeze her tighter.

The vibrations on my phone have long stopped, so I have no doubt the guys are all watching this go down, but she needs to understand.

"When I was ten, he started returning the favour. He'd suck me off and start playing with my ass until he'd force me to feel a release. I didn't understand what was happening, but I felt like shit afterwards. Every time he left, I would feel like I was filthy with his cum all over me or in my stomach." I swallow the clog of emotion in my throat and keep going. "It didn't take him too long to officially take me. God, the pain, Haliee. The fucking pain and shame I felt was unbearable."

She's sobbing against me now, and part of me

thinks I should stop to save her from the cruelty I had to live through, but I can't. She needs to know the demons that lurk beneath us.

Why we've become the killers we have.

"When we got sent to the group home a few years later, where we met Torren, I decided I would never again let anyone control me. That my pleasure was *mine!* I would never let anyone dominate or control me again, but I was addicted to the feeling of release. Instead of being disgusted by it like I did when he forced it from my body over and over again, I felt liberated. I was finally in complete control of my shit." I sigh, taking a deep breath.

"Corden?"

I breathe out against her head. "Yeah, baby?" She pulls back, tears streaking down her beautiful face, looking so sad for the child version of me.

"Can I kiss you?" I suck in a breath, stunned by her question. I feel like I've been gut punched.

After everything I've told her and confessed just now, she still wants to touch me?

"Yeah," I clear my throat. "Yeah, you can always touch and kiss me, baby girl."

She leans in, her eyes open as her soft lips take mine.

I groan into the kiss, never pushing her for more

than the movement of our lips together as I stare into her eyes. They're filled with a love and acceptance I think I've been longing for my whole life.

The second her tongue touches my lips, our eyes close and my hand goes to the back of her neck as I let her in. Our tongues touch, and we both groan as she leans into me, wrapping her arms tightly around my neck as the kiss deepens, but still stays soft.

I could get lost in the feel of her.

Pulling back, I feel a little high as I take her in.

"Thank you for trusting me, Cord."

I swallow and nod, having lost my voice for a second. "Thank you for not reacting badly."

She gives me a huge smile, pulling me into a hug, whispering the sweetest thing I've ever heard. Just for her and I.

"It's okay to have nightmares, Cord. I will hold you and scare them all away for you."

Brent
Chapter Twenty-Three

This town is so full of gossip.

Before I even got home last night, rumours were running about Haliee being in a relationship with seven men.

News to me! As far as I was aware, she was only with Lukas, but I trust her judgement.

If my daughter wants to date seven men, that is her prerogative. Even if it makes me slightly sick to my stomach knowing she's not my innocent little girl anymore. That the little girl I have spent my life protecting and became a killer for, has found her own way in the world and found true love.

Jesus Christ, though!

No father wants to hear that their daughter is

getting intimate with any guy, let alone seven. Not to mention the rumours surrounding those seven.

We've been here for a few months, and the mention of the Deadly Seven is like a whispered myth across this town.

I just happen to know they're true because of the little that Lukas had confessed to me.

Seems taking out the trash means getting rid of rapists and pedophiles, and people who like to beat on women, and that is perfectly fine by me.

If there was any indication that they did something to hurt the innocent, then I would have had Haliee out of here quicker than they could catch us.

She's safe, though, and that's the only thing I've ever wanted.

I've seen the way every single one of those walking erections looks at my daughter. I may not like the lust I see in their eyes, but I admire the complete love and devotion that comes out stronger.

Except Creed. That kid is a creepy son of a bitch, but his obsession with my kid is clear so I let it slide.

Hell, if I had to guess, that sperm scare in her room was probably his psychotic ass and Lukas knew it too. It's why we haven't heard a single thing back from the supposed tests.

Should I be pissed? I am, because that's a sick move for anyone, but having seen Creed recently? It fits.

Now comes the hard part.

Storming into her bedroom and essentially scaring the shit out of the guys to make sure their loyalties are where they need to be.

"Haliee!" I bark, shocking them both out of a sound sleep wrapped in each other's arms.

I'm not an idiot. I know she's been struggling to sleep since Lukas hasn't been around and that's why they all wind up in her bed in the middle of the night.

I know for a fact they all start off on the floor until I hear her soft cries, and I'm grateful she has them, really, I am. But I won't allow them to think I'm okay with just crawling into my daughter's bed like a revolving fucking door.

The kid, Corden, jumps out of the bed like there's a fire on his ass, instantly on the defensive. He doesn't even hesitate to block Haliee from me and my chest swells with pride.

My kid did good.

"Dad? What the hell?!" she screeches, and I

have to keep my face from breaking out in a smile. I love that she's found her fire again.

"Sir, it's not what it looks like," Corden pleads with his eyes, his hands in the air like he's trying to pacify a wild animal.

"Not what it looks like? So, you're not half naked in my daughter's bed when she's dating another man? You know...your supposed brother." His face contorts like someone punched him before Haliee shoves her way past him.

"Dad. We were sleeping and Lukas is fully aware of anything and everything that happens in this room. He has cameras in here to watch over me when I'm sleeping because he can't be here."

Huh, that's a new one. Should be pissed, but it's always good to have eyes watching at all times. Dimitri is a slippery fuck, and he likes to attack in the middle of the night.

He always hopes he will catch us with our guard down, but he doesn't, and he won't.

"You think I don't know who the seven of you are? That I don't know your reputations?" I scoff, looking the kid dead in the eyes. "And you...you think I haven't heard about how much of a whore you are?"

His face pales of colour and I actually feel like

an asshole. Clearly this is a sensitive topic for him, but I don't react. I don't show remorse.

If he is going to get involved with my daughter, he better know to never fucking hurt her. I've killed a lot of men for less over the years.

"Mr. Morgan, I promise you," He chokes on emotion as his eyes swing down to Haliee, and I can tell he's in love with her. "Haliee is different than any other girl I've ever met."

"You're Lust. You expect me to believe that?" I bark and he sighs, looking like a kicked puppy. Haliee goes on the defensive, ready to tear my ass a new one, but I'm not done, so I stop her. "Lukas and the others should be here any minute. Get some clothes on and meet me down there. Now."

I walk out the door, catching him pulling Haliee into his arms and her comforting him.

I just hope this doesn't make her hate me.

Lukas is in the house with the rest of them when I get to the bottom of the stairs, and he looks scared shitless.

"Sir," he says, and I narrow my eyes at him.

"Don't even think about spewing some shit at me about how sharing my daughter is okay," I snap, and he swallows roughly.

"It's not like that," he points out and I laugh without humour.

"So, the fact that the psychotic fuck publicly claimed her as belonging to all of you yesterday, isn't true."

He lets out a strangled breath. "I'm honestly not sure. We've left this completely up to Haliee, but you know her. She's incredible and we all love her so damn much that I feel selfish keeping her for myself if it isn't what *she* wants." He puts emphasis on it being her decision, and I nod.

"It is always going to be about what she wants. If that's every member of the Deadly Seven, so be it. But if you push her, I will kill all of you without hesitation."

He curses under his breath and the giant one, Mathias, stands up. He's a tall bastard and usually pretty quiet, so this should be interesting.

"Every single one of us cares for her, and we're just watching out for her." His eyes narrow on me and if I were a lesser man, I'd be terrified. As it is, I've seen too much shit trying to protect Haliee. "And I think you know that. I think if you had any real fear that she was in danger of being hurt in any way, you'd be a lot angrier than you are right now."

Astute fucker, isn't he? "Come again?" I say instead, not ready to give myself away yet.

"Let's say it a different way since you're being bullheaded about this." He crosses his arms, and I have respect for him not being afraid of me. "You saw me holding Haliee the other night."

I did. Didn't think he knew that though. "Point?"

He runs his hand down his face in annoyance before sharing a look with the guys. I see a few of them nodding at him before he continues.

"I haven't touched, or let a single person touch me, in years. Aside from the very rare time I join in on the things we do, I don't do touch."

I blink. "You don't do touch unless you're beating the shit out of someone before you kill them."

"And he barely does that. He's only ever joined in the physical parts of that a few times," Lukas points out.

"Then why did you touch her?" I think I know why, but I need him to say it.

"Because she needed me. I would never do anything to hurt her, and her cries gutted me."

He sits back down, and I swallow hard, looking

around at the six of them as Haliee and Corden come up behind me.

"I won't leave again, Dad. This is where I belong. Where we belong. Please don't make me leave," she begs and I'm stunned into silence.

She thinks I'm going to make her leave? Fuck no.

She's the safest she's ever been and she's happy. I'd never take that away from her.

From us.

"Sparrow, I'm not making you leave." I take a deep breath and pull her into me. "I'm just worried about this....thing you have with these men," I wince, and she sighs.

"Eagle, the only one I've been intimate with is Luke."

Oh, God. "Nope. Don't want to know. I need a fucking drink." Creed cackles like the lunatic he is, and I narrow my eyes on them. "Anyone hurts her, and I will fuck you up." My eyes move to Corden. He still looks like someone broke him and I feel kind of bad. "And if she chooses to be with all of you, she better be the only choice each of you make." I walk off to the kitchen, but I can still hear them as I pour a glass of scotch.

"Angel, I'm so sorry my shit has caused problems for you," I hear Corden say, and my kid growls.

"Cord, there is nothing you've done wrong and believe me when I say this," I hear her take a deep breath, "I wouldn't have kissed you last night if I believed you were going to go whoring around on me. Don't let your past ruin your future."

Fuck. Make it two drinks. I really should stop eavesdropping.

The less I know about her sex life, the happier we'll all be.

Haliee
Chapter Twenty-Four

After the whole debacle with Dad, Lukas and I have spent the day being lazy and having a movie marathon.

Usually, I leave the lazy days for Sunday, but it's Saturday so…close enough. Not like I could have asked Dad for a drink after admitting that I've had sex with Lukas.

Fuck, that was rough.

Laying tangled up with Lukas is the best way to make me feel happy and at peace, and I will take as much of it as I can.

I fucking missed having him in my bed with me.

He's rubbing small circles around my thigh,

making it hard to concentrate on whatever we're watching.

"I'm sorry about this morning, Scratch. I feel like this situation is my fault for not talking with Brent sooner about all this," Lukas rumbles, bringing it up for the first time since we locked ourselves away.

"It's not your fault, babe. I'm normally more upfront with Dad on everything going on in my life from before we got here, so it's a conversation I should have had with him before now. He doesn't like being surprised if you couldn't tell," I say back.

"I am very aware of that. It still should have gone differently," Lukas growls in anger at himself for us ending up in that situation.

"It's not every day your daughter tells you about multiple boyfriends, Lukas. It's not a conversation you can just bring up over dinner," I sass back.

"Oh yeah? I'm not even going to lie and say I wasn't concerned for my life there for a second when I got here this morning," Lukas replies playfully, rolling over on top of me. "I was just terrified you'd changed your mind and were getting ready to leave me because you finally realized the man I am," he whispers, looking into my eyes with an intensity that makes my breath catch.

"You're the first person I've ever been able to trust besides my father. I don't want shit to go sideways if this isn't real, Lukas. Your rage the other day scared me ,yes, but you haven't lied to me about anything, so I believe the man you say you are. And that is good, whether you have to do some questionable things or not," I whisper, holding his gaze.

He leans down and gently kisses me with such tenderness it makes my heart race.

He moves his hand up my side under my tank top, and rubs his thumb against my rib cage. I was already hot and achy from him teasing me most the day, so I'm instantly wet from just that simple touch.

"Can I make love to you, Haliee?" Lukas whispers against my lips.

I spread my legs a little further apart, giving him an open invitation, and he settles deeper into me while claiming my lips again.

He moves his mouth from mine, down my jaw and starts lifting my tank top off.

"No bra?" he questions with a smirk.

"I knew we weren't going anywhere today, and I wanted to be comfortable," I say, lifting up and tossing my top to the side.

"Sure you weren't just expecting me?" he asks, taking his own shirt off.

"Ego much?" I sass at him again while staring at his sculptured body. He laughs because he knows he's got me.

Dropping back down, he takes my lips again but he's all business now. He reaches down and pops the button on my shorts, and starts trailing kisses down my chest and stomach.

He lifts up slightly, pulling off my shorts and panties with one quick move.

The look he gives me as I lay naked before him makes me feel like a goddess. The heat in his eyes is so intense.

He moves further down the bed and lifts my leg to rest on his shoulder, and starts trailing kisses up my thigh.

He lifts my other leg and repeats the process until he reaches the v between my legs.

Holding my gaze, he opens his mouth and sweeps his tongue across my folds before swirling it around my clit, causing my body to jolt from the sensation.

He grabs my hip to anchor me to him. Still holding my gaze, he starts to suck on my clit, making my back arch and a breathy moan leave my throat.

Moving his tongue back down to my dripping centre and back up to my clit, he repeats the process and has me in a frenzy before I can form a coherent thought.

I feel the cliff fast approaching and move my fist to my mouth to bite down and muffle the scream bubbling up in my chest.

Right before I dive over that blissful peek, he pulls back and gets up to strip his jeans.

"As much as I want you to cum on my face, baby, I need to be inside of you more," he groans out before crawling back up my body. He gives my nipples a bite before claiming my mouth again, letting me taste myself.

"Scratch? Are you on anything? I want to feel you around me with nothing between us," Lukas asks, looking in my eyes with seriousness. "I've never not used a condom with anyone but you. I don't want anything between us because you're different. God, you're everything." He swallows, blushing a little.

Shit. That's cute.

"I've never been on birth control, Luke. It was a way to trace my whereabouts…and before you, I had never even kissed anyone," I reply back honestly, taking a deep breath. "But I need to feel you, Lukas. Please."

"I can get a condom. You do not have to do this. I want you to know that, and I don't want you to feel pressured into doing something you're not comfortable with," Lukas says, pulling back to go for his pants.

I reach out and grab his hand back.

"I want this, Lukas. I want this with you. It's stupid and reckless sure, but my period is due in a couple of days, so I'm well out of my ovulation window," I tell him.

"If you're sure, Scratch. Do not feel pressured because of me," Lukas says, holding my gaze.

My sweet, thoughtful man.

"I'm sure. This is my decision, Lukas," I say, holding his gaze so he understands that I fully comprehend what's about to happen.

I'm dizzy at this point when he lifts my leg around his hip and nudges my opening with his hard length, slowly gliding into me. His other hand moves to the back of my head and grabs a fist full of hair to gain access to my neck.

I dig my hands into his back as mine arches from his raw and hot length filling me to the brim.

We both release a breathy moan as he starts slowly working his cock in and out of my channel, hitting that perfect spot each time, building me back up again.

It doesn't take long until I'm close to the edge of the orgasm he stopped earlier.

This time, though, it's more intense.

"I love you, Scratch. So goddamn much," he moans, coming back in to kiss me.

"Lukas" I whisper, trying to reply back but he thrusts into me again, harder than before and stealing my voice from me.

He starts to pick up speed and reaches down with the hand that was in my hair, strumming my clit like it's the instrument he's spent years dedicated to mastering.

My head thrashes back and forth, trying my hardest to hold back my volume because I don't want to give Dad any more reason to lose it on me today, but Lukas is making it impossible.

"Cum for me, baby. Let me feel you squeeze me," Lukas says, his thrusts fast and short with deep strokes, hitting that insane place deep inside me with every pass.

I couldn't hold back the orgasm if I tried. It hits

me so hard I almost black out for a second as pleasure consumes me.

Sweat is clinging to our skin and our hearts are almost in sync, racing out our chests.

He's still thrusting lazily as I start coming down from the high of the tidal wave that just hit me, while he looks at me in awe.

"God, baby, you're so fucking beautiful when you cum around my dick," he moans out, and picks up his pace again.

His poor back is going to look so clawed tomorrow, but right now I don't care because he's starting to work me up again.

I feel his thrusts start to falter a bit as he reaches his own peak, but I'm right there with him again just as fast. This one isn't as intense as the last, but it still sends shivers up my spine.

"Baby. Fuck. Fuck. Fuck," Lukas starts chanting as his cock throbs in me with his release. He thrusts one last time, holding still for a second before pulling out of me.

He reaches down and runs to fingers across my opening before slowly inserting them inside. I moan again when a look of possessiveness crosses his face at feeling his release inside me.

He pushes my legs open and watches his cum drips around his fingers and out of me.

When he looks back up at me, an odd look crosses his face confusing me.

"What?" I ask, starting to become embarrassed.

"This is the hottest thing I've ever seen in my life, baby, but I got to be honest with you. Seeing my cum leak out of you makes me want to get you pregnant so I can tie you to me forever. Corden's not the only one that's selfish. We all are. But watching a life grow inside you that I put there… Scratch, you make me want shit we shouldn't do right now," Lukas says, looking at me and watching my reaction.

That's a lot to process. I've never thought about children before, but now that he's putting a voice to it, I may be crazy because I kind of like the idea.

"Maybe in the future when things aren't so crazy, Lukas. Now would be a horrible time for us both," I say with all honesty. I think I would love to have kids with him, and even the other guys if we're going to be a solid family…but not until Dimitri has been removed from my life permanently.

I refuse to ever put a child in that kind of danger.

"Really? You'd think about having my baby, Haliee?" Lukas asks, finally releasing me and leaning down to kiss me.

"Yeah, Lukas. Maybe someday," I say after we break apart. He lays down and holds me to his chest as we catch our breath, stroking my hair while we just lay there lost in thought.

"Let's go get cleaned up and get some rest," Lukas says after a while, kissing the top of my head.

Dimitri
Chapter Twenty-Five

This game is becoming tiresome.

It was fun to chase her for a while, letting her father get the upper hand because, contrary to what some may believe, I didn't buy Haliee because she was a child.

I bought her because she was a mini replica of her mother, and damn if that woman wasn't fine...for a whore.

Haliee, however, is much different from that cunt, and I knew she would be. I knew she would be sweet and innocent, and stunning to look at.

A light in the dark world I rule with an iron fist.

I think she believes her mother is still alive, but she isn't.

I couldn't let someone live who was willing to sell their only child to a devil in order to save themselves. I may be a monster, but I've always had one rule I live and breathe by.

We do not harm children.

I would have raised Haliee to be strong and independent, but to also be soft for me, and me alone.

She deserved better than a life on the run, never being able to settle down and be herself, and I will give that to her.

It will take time for her to realize I have only ever wanted to give her the world, but she will. She won't have another choice.

She's mine.

But now that she's been tainted, I've lost my patience.

She is mine!

I'm pissed beyond belief I didn't get her innocence, but she is still relatively untouched...unless those other men start playing with what is mine as well.

I'm finished with her father ignoring my threats because he knows I can't get to her.

Bad luck, that. Her having to fall for the Deadly Seven.

I've done my research and they are most definitely a group you should steer clear of, but I can't. They've taken what belongs to me, and I want her back.

I want to make her see that she was meant to be mine, and I can give her everything she has ever wanted.

They may be guarding her tighter than Fort fucking Knox, but I am Dimitri Koschov. I don't back down from anyone, least of all a group of unruly children who seem to think they're badasses.

I will take her from them one way or another, and if that means making her come to me? Fine.

The Deadly Seven have never come up against a true threat...until now.

Haliee
Chapter Twenty-Six

You know that feeling in the pit of your stomach when you know a storm is coming your way?

I've had it for a few days now, and it only means one thing.

Dimitri is coming for me.

I've been doing this song and dance long enough to almost have a sixth sense about it. It's hard to explain, but these small things change leading up to his deciding to make a move.

I feel like I'm being watched again, but I know it's not the guys. I know it's someone from his team because my entire body is a live wire ready to explode.

I constantly feel dirty and exposed, and that was never a problem from my guys. Even when I first came here, I never felt so violated or creeped out.

Aside from the sperm ordeal, but I'm beginning to think it was Creed behind that disgusting night. It just screams his psychosis.

I need to remember and ask him outright if it was him so I can put that to rest, but for now I have other things to worry about.

Looking outside my window, I can't make out anyone who could be out of place, but that's not uncommon either. I've never seen his men before they attack, I just feel them.

Fuck, listen to me losing my mind. I'm talking about having some sort of psychic connection to the man who claims he owns me, like I'm a piece of property to him.

Luke is downstairs with Dad and their conversation is getting heated.

We know Dad is hiding something from us because he's been distant recently. He's always trying to make an excuse to be away from us, away from me, and it just lends to this fucking feeling I have.

Pulling my phone out of my sweater pocket, I dial Ollie.

"Hey, Angel, everything alright?" he asks, his sweet voice bringing a small smile to my face.

"Hey, nerd," I tease him and he chuckles. "How are you guys over there?" I sit down on the bed, letting Hope climb into my lap and ease some of the tension.

I love her so damn much, and I will always love Matty for getting her for me.

"We're alright. Doing better than you by the looks of it. What's wrong, Angel?" I narrow my eyes, looking around the room for any indication of where that damn camera may be, and he cackles on the other end. "You won't find it. Tell me what's wrong, Angel."

I swallow, tears burning the back of my eyes. "Something is off, Ollie."

"Explain, please." His voice went from playful to serious in under a second and I sigh.

"You're going to think I'm crazy," I whine, and he growls.

"Haliee Morgan, don't you dare try and get out of this. What do you mean something is off? Are you sick?"

I snort, wishing it was that simple. "I wish it was something like that." I take a deep breath, petting

Hope's head. "I've spent most of my life running from Dimitri, Ollie."

"I know, Angel. So why don't you tell me what is on your mind so I can help? It's why you called me instead of someone else."

I whimper and nod, batting the lone tear off my cheek like it offends me. "They're here, Ollie. I can feel them watching me." I push forward through my clogged throat.

"You always have eyes on you right now."

I sigh, knowing it was stupid and no one would believe me.

Well, Dad would, but he would instantly toss us in the car and disappear faster than we arrived, and I just don't have the fucking energy to run anymore.

"Tell me what makes this feeling different," he asks, and I want to cry at how soft his voice is.

"Every time he's close, I feel eyes on me but it's not like when you guys were watching me." I choke out a cry. "I feel exposed and violated. Like I need to have a shower and hide away in the darkness just to get their vile eyes off of me. Ollie, I know it's crazy, but it happens every time," I plead with him to understand.

I hear a bunch of noise coming from their end of the line before a door slams.

"I believe you, Angel. Let me do some recon and see if I can find anyone suspicious. Do you feel it right now?"

I swallow, getting up and looking out my window again. The shivers of fear and panic run through me and I want to scream. "They're outside, Ollie, I just know it."

I'm full-blown crying now, and he growls.

"I'm going to look, Angel, but that means I need to let you go in case I have to call Luke. Creed is already on his way there to stay with you. You know he will kill anyone who even tries to come near you."

I nod my head. "I know. Thank you for believing me, Ollie."

He grunts. "Always, Angel," he says before the line disconnects.

I take a deep breath as the shouting gets louder downstairs.

What the hell could they possibly be fighting about right now?

Opening the door, I catch the tail end of Dad's angry voice.

"You lied to her! You don't think she's going to be pissed about that?!" he shouts, and Lukas curses.

"Of course she's going to be pissed, but what good would it have made to bring it up once I knew the truth? By the time I knew for certain, it had been weeks! She had all but forgotten about it."

Dad scoffs and I swallow hard. "You really think she could ever forget that? She was terrified, and you knew all along that she was never in danger. That's on you."

Wait…

"I know Creed fucked up, but she knows what he's like. She'll understand." Luke doesn't sound so certain, and truthfully? Neither am I.

I let Lukas in because I trusted him to be honest with me and he lied.

How can I trust anything he's said and done to this point if he lied to me from the beginning?

Am I pissed Creed jacked off into my bed and ran? Watched me bathe naked and get myself off?

Fucking right I am! But I'm more upset that Lukas could have erased those fears a long time ago and he didn't.

Oh, God, Creed is coming here right now.

I can't take this fighting or seeing any of them right now. It's too fucking much.

Running back up to my room, I grab my jacket before climbing out the window and running into the trees behind the house.

Oliver

I FEEL my heart beating in my throat. Haliee was somehow right. There are men in the fucking woods around her house that seem to have popped out of thin fucking air.

And she just took the fuck off out there.

Brent and Lukas have no clue as they continue their heated discussion, and whatever they're discussing set her off to the point she ran.

She fucking ran from the house.

Alone.

I feel desperate as I dial her phone over and over just to have it go through to voicemail. This can't be happening. Everything was set up to perfection to prevent this shit from going down, but here we fucking are.

We didn't factor in that Haliee would run from us.

The men are getting closer to the house by the

second and I make the split-second choice that I already know will come back to bite me in the ass.

God, Haliee fucking forgive me.

I pick my phone back up and patch through to Creed's Bluetooth earpiece, turning my back on the monitor watching Lukas and Brent.

Haliee is my first priority.

"Did me not bending you over before I left not get you off enough?" Creed answers so crassly.

"Code Angel! We have rats crawling everywhere and the Sparrow has flown the fucking coop! Due south. Fifteen minutes out. FUCKING RUN, CREED!" I roar back, letting the desperation leak out with every word.

"Copy," comes his reply as I hear him abandon his bike and take off on foot so he doesn't alert the uninvited guests.

I keep my eyes locked on Haliee moving through the woods looking desperate to escape while having no clue the danger she's sunk herself into.

Watching the camera feeds as well as her tracker, I make sure to scream the directions to Creed so he goes the right way.

I watch the moment she realizes she's not as

alone in the woods as she believed herself to be, and feel sick to my stomach.

A man in tactical gear steps out from behind the tree and she lets out a scream I know everyone can hear.

I can hear it from here and my video feed is fucking silent.

I watch Creed zoom through the woods getting closer and closer to her.

"FUCKING LEFT, CREED!" I blare out, keeping him on the right path to her.

He twists with the lethal grace of a natural born killer and keeps his speed, drawing closer.

I watch helplessly as the man in tactical gear taunts our Angel, rumbling out a laugh I see in his chest at her terror filled expression.

Creed slows his pace, finally coming up on them and drawing out his favourite blade.

The man has no clue the demon lingering behind him, and I send up a silent thank you to whatever deity is listening as I watch Creed creep up on him, grabbing his forehead from behind and slicing this throat in one smooth move.

Haliee screams again at the sight of Creed's demon fully unleashed, and turns to run from him.

No bother now, though. Creed has this handled.

I twist back toward Brent's monitor and my heart sinks as I watch men in tactical gear dragging his unconscious body through the woods.

FUCK! LUKAS!

I start flicking monitor after monitor looking for any sign of him when hope fills my chest at the sight of him taking out two of the men headed in Haliee's direction.

He must have heard the scream and went for her.

Hold on, Brent. We will find you.

Brent
Epilogue

Moments earlier...

HE CAN'T BE this fucking dense.

How can he be twenty-eight and not realize how vulnerable Haliee is going to be to his omission?

"I know you kept it from her because he's your brother, but she won't see it like that," I spit at him, and he groans.

"Fuck. I was just trying to do what was best for everyone. I stopped thinking about it as soon as

Creed admitted it," he admits, dropping into a chair with a look of defeat. "How am I going to tell her the truth?" he asks me, and I shake my head.

"Rip the band-aid off, kid. It's the only choice you have. Tell her the truth and deal with the consequences of your own actions."

He swallows. "I was just trying to protect her."

I sigh, sitting down across from him. "I don't know what to tell you, Lukas. You're a smart kid and you love my daughter, but she's not going to see that at first."

"She's going to see the lie and feel like nothing between us was real." His voice cracks and I sigh, nodding.

I go to speak, but his phone dings and he pulls it out. I know it's one of the brothers texting because he never ignores that sound.

"What the—" He's cut off by a shrill scream coming from the woods, and my blood runs cold.

"Haliee!" we both scream, jumping up and racing to the door.

"You go that way!" I point to the right and he nods.

"Keep your eyes open and your phone on. We'll find her, but this could be a trap." I swallow the fear down and nod before we make our way to opposite ends of the forest. I needed to get him away from me because I know this is a trap.

I don't know how they got her out of the house, but I do know that Dimitri's men have arrived, and I can't let anything happen to her.

I shouldn't have ignored his threats, but I did so because I knew she would be safe. She was finally happy and living a good life, I didn't want to rip that away from her just because he was threatening me.

"Haliee!" I scream into the cold air. "Where are you, Sparrow?!" I shout again, but nothing.

I can vaguely hear Lukas screaming out for her and I just hope he finds her.

I'm pulling out my phone to call him when something hits me hard and I fall to the ground, dropping my phone in the snow.

My vision is blurry, but I see a shadowed figure bending down in front of me.

"Took you long enough. Dimitri would like to see you."

It's the last thing I hear before everything goes black.

THE END FOR NOW...

. . .

Book 2: *Seduction* **coming January 24, 2022!**

Pre-Order Seduction HERE

Sneak Peak at Trick or Revenge

BY CASSIE HARGROVE

Trick or Revenge (A Standalone RH)

Prologue – *The Golden Boys*

Have you ever wanted something you couldn't have?

The four of us, the Golden Boys of Freemont High, we are all in love with the same girl and she wants nothing to do with us.

We made it that way to protect her.

No one touches her or even acknowledges her in any way. She's a loner, an outcast in society.

It's better to be invisible, than to fall prey to the sharks that would love nothing more than to taint her soul.

One day, when we are free and clear of this town, we will make her ours.

Until then, we keep her safe by making sure we are the only ones to interact with her. See, we claimed her as our own personal toy and made it known that no one else was to touch her. And what we want, we get.

We bully her every day to make sure she keeps her head down and out of trouble. If she's upset and depressed, she won't go looking in the places she doesn't belong, and that keeps her safe.

But if anyone hurts her?

We have a secret that no one knows…

Be careful who you cross, because the Golden Boys of Freemont High aren't nearly as golden as everyone thinks.

Chapter 1 – *Carly*

Another year in this hell and I'm leaving, never to return to this place that's become my own personal nightmare.

Even before the events of this summer, I knew staying here wasn't an option. I don't fit in with this place or the people and they've made that more than clear. Not that I would want to fit in with anyone who seems to think they're untouchable gods, but even one friend could have made all the difference.

I'm okay with not belonging here and it's not like I will miss my parents either. They do belong here, and they are loved by everyone. I'm the daughter they wished they had never had, and if we aren't out in public, I don't exist to them.

I've always been quiet and liked to keep to myself. I have no interest in the vain world my parents choose to live in, so I ignore it. All of it, and I'm happier with myself that way.

At least when I look at myself in the mirror, it's not filled with self-hatred for being a self-centred bitch.

I was fourteen when we moved here and life hasn't been easy, but I've never given up. I bide my time and don't fight back. I take the bullying as it comes.

And it does come…from the four hottest most coveted guys in town.

The Golden Boys.

Such a stupid fucking name, but they come from the four founding families of Wilmington. Their families own everything around us, and they make sure everyone knows it and it makes them untouchable.

Before this summer, I could take their shit without batting an eyelash.

Now? Now I'm afraid they might actually break me if they push too hard.

I'm on the edge of a cliff, ready to fall into the darkness and let it swallow me whole. If they come at me with their usual intensity, I'm fucked. I know I am.

There's only so much one girl can take.

"There she is." I hold in the groan as I hear Bishop's velvety voice wash over me. Closing my eyes, I take a deep breath and remind myself that this isn't anything I can't handle. I've dealt with them for three years. No matter what happened to me this summer, I know I can handle *them*. I just need to lock everything away to get through it.

Just a few more months.

"Awe, we missed you Care Bear." Mark purrs from somewhere closer and I stiffen my shoulders, refusing to let them fuck me up on the first day. "Summer is never the same without you."

I'm fine. I've got this.

I take a step away and feel a hand land on my shoulder and jolt.

Nope. No fucking way. They can taunt me and knock me down, but they can't touch me.

Shaking them off, I make my way to the classroom, not even looking to see whose hand gripped me.

I don't care which of them it was, because if I have my way, no one will ever fucking touch me again.

I take a seat in the back corner of the classroom and breathe a sigh of relief as I look around. Maybe I will be lucky and not share a class with any of them. Just this once, the universe may be giving me a pass.

My happiness is short lived as Evan Phelps walks in, taking stock of the room before narrowing his eyes in on the empty seat beside me.

No, God no. Please, anywhere but here.

I lay my head in my arms and groan as he makes his way over here with a smirk on his all too handsome face.

It would be nice if the universe quit shitting on me. Even just for one miserable damn day because lately, she's been a miserable cunt I'd like to stab.

I have never done anything to deserve the shit she's thrown at me the past couple months.

"Well, isn't this a nice surprise. You don't usually sit back here." The chair beside me screeches across the floor as he flops into it and I sigh, lifting my head but refusing to acknowledge him.

This is all my fault.

It's my mistake that gave him the free access to sit beside me. I wanted to disappear into the background even more than I have in the past, and that just gave him the ammunition he needed to taunt me some more. Fucking perfect.

The bell rings and I bend over to take my books out for homeroom as the teacher walks into the classroom and closes the door.

"Good morning, everyone. My name is Mr. Granger." Everyone around us mumbles something, but I don't pay any attention. I keep my head and eyes on my books as not to give the evil spawn beside me more ammunition.

Okay, to be fair, Evan is the nicest of the four of them, but he's still a dick. To his credit, he must sense my unwillingness to deal with his shit, and he doesn't say much as the teacher goes through roll call to make sure we're all in attendance.

I keep my eyes on my books, doodling something in the corner of one of my notebooks when my name is called.

"Carly Harrison." The sound of my name snaps me out of my daze, and I pull my head up.

"Here." I state as I look at our new teacher and forget how to breathe.

His cold eyes hold mine with a darkness I remember well, and I suddenly feel dizzy as I take in the satisfied smirk that appears on his face.

"New teacher." Evan pulls tighter into the desk and whispers under his breath. I don't answer him. I don't take my eyes off the teacher in front of us as he continues with the attendance, his eyes never far from mine. "Hey, are you okay? You don't look like you're breathing." He asks with genuine concern in his voice, but I can't respond.

I'm frozen in the fear, reliving the worst night of my life as I see those haunting eyes staring at me with lust. This can't be happening.

"Fine." I croak, remembering to breathe thanks to Evan's timely reminder.

My lungs burn as they welcome the oxygen I was depriving them of while my brain had short circuited.

He narrows his eyes like he doesn't believe me, and I want to roll my eyes at him and not give anything away just like any other time one of them has seen me vulnerable, but I can't.

I can't play this off as nothing when my brain is a complete mess.

Him and I both know I lied by saying I'm fine, but I refuse to give him anything else. My trauma is none of his concern.

"Today is going to be simple. I want to go over your syllabus with you and answer any questions you may have. If we have time afterwards, I'd love the chance to get to know you guys and give you the same courtesy."

Mr. Granger starts walking around the room, handing out packages for the semester, his eyes watching me closely. I can feel them on me, and it makes me want to scratch at my skin to remove his unwanted attention.

If I were anyone else, I wouldn't even notice him doing it because he's that good at hiding it. But I know I feel them because it's the same feeling I had that night that I couldn't shake.

I can't believe how dumb I was. I should have listened to my gut when I felt like I was being watched, but I didn't. I ignored that inner warning that something was wrong, and I paid the price on my way home from work.

A price no one should ever have to pay.

He moves toward us, and I reach out to take the packet from him, trying to steady my breath as my stomach churns with acid from the smell of his cologne.

Cinnamon and Old Spice.

I swallow the bile down as that night comes flooding back, memory by memory. Assaulting me even more than a few moments ago when I looked into his eyes.

I can't do this right now. I have to go.

Standing up, I start throwing my things into my bag.

"Excuse me." I say, not looking at anyone as my eyes start to get blurry. Running out of the classroom, I hurry to the nearest trashcan to empty my stomach.

I stay there, bent over the trashcan, trying to steady my breathing when I hear a door open behind me.

I'm not sure if it's him, or someone else from another class, but I will not stick around to find out. I do the only thing I can think of and run. Because this time, I'm not being held down and I can run.

I run out the doors and don't stop until I reach the quiet park a few blocks from the school and sit down against a tree in the far corner. I'm far enough away from the entrance that no one will find me here. I'm safe and I can breathe.

This isn't happening, it's just a nightmare. This isn't happening, it's just a nightmare.

I repeat the words over and over, begging myself to believe them as I lean against the tree trying to catch my breath…but I know what I saw. *WHO* I saw.

**Coming Oct 26 to Kindle Unlimited
Pre-order Here:**

Acknowledgments

Wow.

This was a wild ride for us from start to finish!

Cassie Hargrove:

When Story first reached out to me about writing a dark romance together, I was all for it. Not even the slightest hesitation came to mind because I knew her mind was brilliant.

What I didn't know was that we would end up coming up with the entire concept of this series while completely drunk on our asses (shhh it's a secret) hahahah.

This girl has been my ride or die in the book world for months now and I absolutely love the hell out of her. I couldn't imagine doing a project like this with anyone else.

I kid you not, most of the time it was like we

shared a brain and it was kind of creepy, but in the absolute best ways possible.

Thank you do much for taking the time to read our crazy ideas and we hope you enjoyed it! Now it's time for us to dive into book 2 so we can bring you more of Haliee and her guys!

Story Brooks:

Oh boy! Where do I begin!

For my debut I could not be more grateful to Cassie for holding my hand and being the absolute rock star she is with all the hours and work put into this book.

She's become a second pair of wings guiding me on how to fly.

I cannot be thankful enough to the readers that pick up this book and dive into this story(hehe). Without you there would be no book!

Thank you for taking this journey with us and hang in there k? We will make it better……hopefully.

About the Authors

Cassie Hargrove has been writing romance for the past year and a half while living her best life from home.

She lives with her husband and three kids, a dog and three cats and is quite literally the ring leader in her crazy circus.

She's always enjoyed reading and writing and loves that so many readers are enjoying her work.

Story Brooks is a full time mom and wife while working from home helping others live their best lives.

This is the first time she's written anything to publish, but she's always had a passion for reading and writing that just never quit.

Also by Cassie Hargrove

Suited Up Daddies

1: Daddy's Naughty Secretary

2: Daddy's Little Novice

3: Daddy's Proper Present

4: Daddy's Precious Rose

5: Daddy's Sexy Sub

6: Daddy's Perfect Pair (Coming Dec 20/21)

Connerton Academy (A Complete Series)

(A Paranormal Reverse Harem Romance)

1: Freshman Firsts

2: Sophomore Secrets

3: Junior Lessons in Justice

4: Senior Sacrifices

Serenity Stables

(A Daddies and Doms Series)

1: The Freedom of Safety

2: The Feeling of Home

Forbidden Kinks

1: Still Part 1 (Part 2 Coming Soon)

Erotic Shorts

Taken By Him

Intern-al Affairs

Bound to Him

Made in the USA
Middletown, DE
10 January 2023